THE FAMILY FIASCO

Anna Wilson

Illustrated
by
Nicola Kinnear

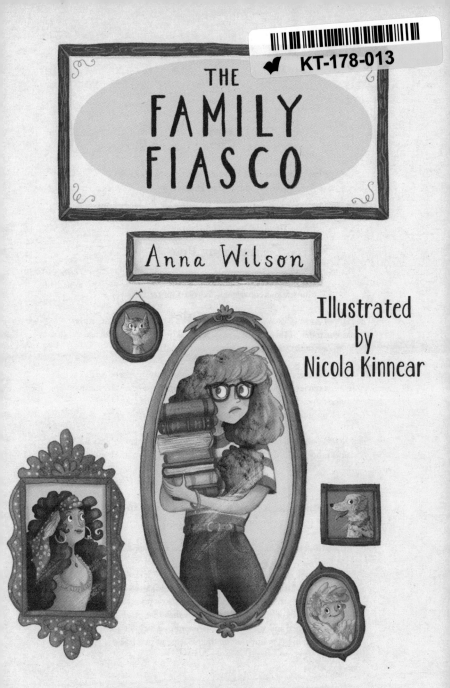

MACMILLAN CHILDREN'S BOOKS

First published 2017 by Macmillan Children's Books
an imprint of Pan Macmillan
20 New Wharf Road, London N1 9RR
Associated companies throughout the world
www.panmacmillan.com

ISBN 978-1-5098-0129-9

1 3 5 7 9 8 6 4 2

A CIP catalogue record for this book is available from
the British Library.

Printed and bound by CPI Group (UK) Ltd, Croydon CR0 4YY

For David, Lucy and Tom xxx

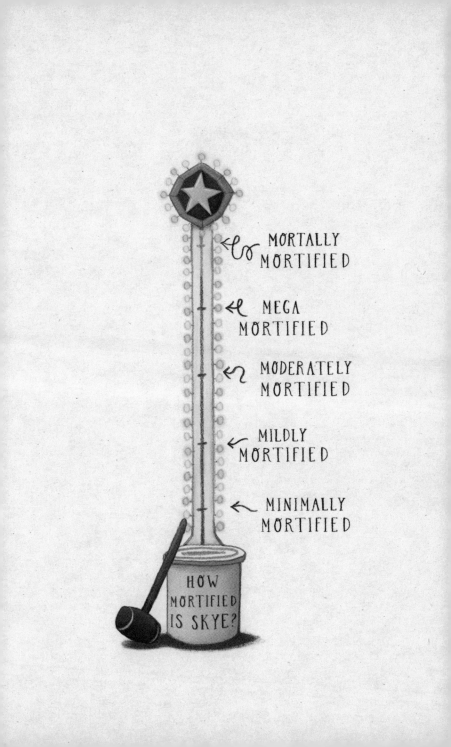

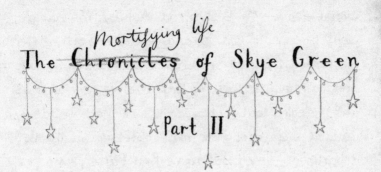

The ~~Mortifying life~~ Chronicles of Skye Green

Part II

I am not looking forward to my birthday.

I know that probably sounds insane. I mean, who doesn't look forward to a birthday? Answer: people who have a mortifying family like mine. Actually, I don't know anyone else in the entire universe whose family is as mortifying as mine. That is why the only place I can admit to not looking forward to my birthday is right here, in my journal. If I said the reasons out loud, no one would understand.

Here they are:

Firstly, I am going to be thirteen, which means, as my mother and little brother are fond of reminding me every five minutes, I am going to be a TEENAGER. From what I have seen, turning teen is not something to which any sensible person would aspire. My best friend Aubrey, for example, went through a very strange episode shortly after she turned thirteen. She became *obsessed* with boys and painting her toes nuclear-reactive neon colours and hanging out with people she had suddenly decided were cool. The main obsession in the boy department turned out to be Finn Parker, who just happens to be my next-door neighbour, and whose dad, Rob, just happens to be dating my mum. Yes, HIDEOUS FACT: just to pile on the mortification to my ever-more mortifying life – MY MUM IS DATING THE MAN NEXT DOOR.

Aubrey almost broke our friendship for good last term over all her teen-tastic try-hard behaviour. This was mainly because of her frankly baffling new choice of friends – in other words the toxic twins, Izzy and Livvy Vorderman (aka the Voldemort Twins, owing to their general evilness, aka the VTs for short).

Luckily, though, I can report that all that is in the past and Aubrey and I are best friends again.

Unluckily Aubrey has been away THE WHOLE summer, so I have had no one to talk to about my fears of turning teen, and she is not here to help me get through the trauma of my birthday, which is apparently going to involve going out for 'a nice family meal'. Without my best friend. Just me, my embarrassing mother and little brother. And Rob. And Finn.

HOW IS THIS IN ANY WAY 'A NICE FAMILY MEAL'?!

For a start, Rob and Finn are not 'family'.

And for a finish, there is nothing 'nice' about my *actual* family.

Mum 'can't understand why I am being so grumpy'. She has a point. After all, we are going to my favourite pizza place and Rob is paying, which is very kind of him. It's not that I have a problem with Rob himself. I have even (sort of) got used to the fact that Mum has a boyfriend. (Although I can't say that out loud - Rob is a man and he has a beard - there is nothing 'boy' about him. Calling him 'Mum's boyfriend' is just WRONG on so many levels!) I have also (kind-of-sort-of) got used to them kissing IN FRONT OF ME. ('Hashtag GROSS!' as Aubrey might say.)

Plus, I would never say this out loud, but I

have actually come to the conclusion that Mum is a lot happier and a much nicer mum now that Rob is in her life.

So the problem is not really Rob.

The problem is that Mum wants us to 'bond' and keeps using the word 'family' in inappropriate contexts, such as in the question, 'Wouldn't it be nice to go out AS A FAMILY for your birthday?'

To which the answer is: NO, IT WOULD NOT.

Hasn't she read any fairy tales? Doesn't she know that bringing families together and making perfect strangers accept one another as brothers and sisters is always a recipe for disaster?

Because Finn being my brother would definitely be that.

The trouble is, Harris thinks Finn Parker is big brotherly perfection itself.

I just wish Aubrey was here. How am I going to survive this without her?

Chapter One

'Here we are, guys!' Rob says. 'Mama Mia's. The best pizza place in the solar system, according to one reviewer.'

'They might be overdoing it slightly,' Finn mutters.

'Yeah, coz like I bet there are AMAZING pizza places on Jupiter!' says Harris, punching the air.

Rob laughs. 'I think Finn meant there just might be better places in Italy?'

Mum grabs Harris and tickles him until he squeals like a piglet. 'What do aliens on Jupiter eat, little bean?'

'Irritating small boys, deep fried in hot oil, I hope,' I say under my breath.

Not for the first time, I wish I had been able to go away with Aubrey. She and her family (as in proper, real family) have gone to New Zealand for the whole summer to have the *Lord of the Rings* 'experience'. They are going to a 'live action battle with real Orcs and everything' today, according to her last text.

When I mentioned this in the car earlier this evening, Finn snorted and said it just went to show what a weirdo my best friend was. I managed to hold back from saying he would know what a weirdo was seeing as he was the biggest one in the history of the entire human race. Surely anyone can see that going for a tour of Middle-earth is the coolest thing ever? It's a lot more exciting than spending your summer listening to Finn practise the drums and 'sharing' the sofa and remote with him and Harris. (Although, to be fair, the drumming at least sounds more like music now and less like a box of badgers attempting to fight their way out.)

We enter the restaurant and wait while Rob explains that we have a reservation. I scan the room for any sign of someone I might know. Like I say, I am fine with Mum and Rob seeing each other, but I would rather not bump into anyone from school. It's just too embarrassing to have to publicly acknowledge that my mum is dating Finn's dad. Plus, what if they kiss and someone from school sees? I would literally die.

I glance at Finn. He is pulling his floppy fringe down over his face and looking shifty. I guess he's not that relaxed about us going out 'as a family' either.

A waiter takes us to our table. Luckily I do not spot anyone I know. The VTs would be the worst. They too have a crush on Finn, plus they are well known for snapping away and posting photos of their whole lives online. It would be just like them to post a photo of us all together with some snidey comment. They did get into trouble for doing this last term, but I do not trust them to have learned their lesson. They could easily post a picture online of Mum and Rob, for example. They only promised not to do this of people at school, e.g. me.

We sit down – Mum and Rob next to each other on a bench, Harris on the end, and Finn and me next to each other (worst luck) – and the waiter gives us menus and takes our drinks order.

'You can choose whatever you like, Skye,' Rob says. 'I want you to have a great time this evening. It's a big deal, turning thirteen.'

'Teenager! Teenager!' Harris chants.

'Shut up, squirt,' I mutter.

Finn lets out one of his trademark sniggers.

'Skye likes lemonade but it makes her burp!' Harris shouts, and then laughs so hard that snot comes out of his nose.

Kill. Me. Now.

'Boys . . .' Mum says, rolling her eyes in mock impatience.

This has been her mantra all holiday. When Harris and Finn were racing through the house having a nerf-gun battle and hitting me between the eyes, giving me a nasty bruise, it was 'Boys . . .' and that eye-roll. When Finn and Harris put milk in the juice carton and juice in the milk carton so that I poured orange juice all over my cereal at breakfast, it was 'Boys . . .' and the eye-roll again. Basically, whenever they do anything irritating or stupid or horrible they get Mum shaking her head in a 'you're so funny' kind of way. But if I do anything at all out of line, such as leaving the butter dish uncovered so that my cat Gollum eats all the butter and is then sick, I get a full-on lecture. (OK, so Pongo the dog did eat the sick and was then sick himself in Mum's favourite pair of DMs – the bubblegum-pink ones – but how is that my fault?)

I decide to concentrate on which pizza I am going to order. The best way to enjoy my birthday is to ignore Finn and Harris, I reckon. I begin reading through the list of pizzas even though I know I will probably go for the one I always choose: ham and cheese and olives with extra chunks of pineapple.

'Skye?' Mum is saying, waving a hand in front of my face. 'Earth calling Skye?'

'Excellent!' says Finn. 'I am so going to use that one. "Earth calling Skye",' he repeats.

Harris whoops with laughter too and chants, 'Earth calling Skye! Earth calling Skye!'

I lower my menu and glower at him.

'Come on, Skye,' says Mum, 'we are all waiting for you to choose. We want to give you your presents.'

'Er, it's OK,' I say. 'I'd rather open them at home later. It's a bit public here.'

I have had some pretty bad presents from Mum in the past, so I really could do without having to act all polite and happy in front of Finn and Rob when Mum goes and gives me a Hello Kitty pencil case. Or worse.

'Don't worry, I haven't got you anything embarrassing!' Mum coos, reading my awkwardness and exposing it for all to see.

'Not like last year when you gave Skye some pants with Minions on!' Harris says, a little too loudly.

The family on the next table pop their heads up like a bunch of meerkats, and Finn's usual snigger erupts into a full-blown gale of laughter.

Mum reaches across Rob and puts her hand on Harris's arm. '*Don't*, Harris,' she says.

The waiter comes back to take our orders and, guess what, I do choose my usual. The conversation turns to what a lovely summer it has been and how great it is that we have spent so much time together.

I let most of it drift over my head. I am thinking about Aubrey and whether or not she has remembered my birthday. It has been too difficult to communicate with her while she is away. Her parents won't let her text me because they say it is too expensive. We can message each other when she is in her hotel room where there is Wi-Fi, but because of the time difference between here and New Zealand our conversations are disjointed: I can only reply when it is her night-time, and vice versa. So when I messaged the other day to say:

> Can't believe it – Finn and Rob here AGAIN. Rob cooking dinner. Mum in über-loved-up-mode. SAVE ME. ☺

I had to wait almost twenty-four hours before a message pinged up saying:

> OMG. That is totally a crime against fashion. ⦿⦿

Which of course made no sense at all until I scrolled back to find she must have replied to an earlier message that I'd sent about what Mum had chosen to wear that day.

It was like a game of 'Answer the Question Before Last'. (There is a clip on YouTube of someone doing this as if they are on the TV quiz show *Mastermind*. It is worth watching, as it is very funny. It is, however, not so funny in real life when you are trying to ask your best friend for advice and sympathy.)

Mum is reaching down under the table. She brings up a package wrapped in shiny paper and tied with a large purple ribbon. She pushes it across the table towards me.

'Happy birthday, lovely daughter,' says Mum.

'Thanks,' I say, smiling. I kind of want to add 'lovely Mum', but I can't quite bring myself to say that. Especially not in front of Finn.

'And Finn and I got you this,' Rob says. He looks shy as he offers another package up from under the table.

I dread to think what Finn might have got me. A whoopee cushion or a fake dog poo? Mind you, if Rob was involved it might be an OK present.

I open Mum's gift first. It is a beautiful leather-bound notebook with a metal clasp, lock and key and a pencil, which slots into a band of leather on the side.

Rob's is an amazing hardcover copy of *Harry Potter and the Philosopher's Stone* in a fancy kind of box that you slide the book in and out of. The book looks old-fashioned with the words stamped in gold straight on to the cover. It feels and smells like the book itself is magical. (Of course, in many ways it is – after all, J. K. Rowling did say, 'I do believe something very magical can happen when you read a good book.' I couldn't agree more.)

Harris then proudly gives me a picture he has drawn of me reading, sitting on my windowsill, which is my favourite place to sit.

I am overwhelmed by how thoughtful everyone has been. Especially Rob. I also feel ashamed of myself for being so grumpy about going out together.

'Thank you so much,' I manage.

How come when I am writing I can think of the words to express how I feel, but when I am faced with trying to speak those words, they just don't come? I would like to say how surprised I am by Rob's choice of present; I would like to ask Finn if he had a hand in it – he is looking unusually happy and not sneering at me for once. Or did Mum put them up to this to try and get me on side? I watch her look at Rob and see him take her hand and squeeze it. I realize that she must have told him what I would like. Has he done this to bribe me?

The pizzas arrive and we tuck in. I am locked in my own thoughts and am not paying much attention to the conversation around me. This happens a lot to me. I get lost in what is going on inside my head, like I am in a dream, then someone says something to me and I snap out of it and realize I have no idea what they have just said. Mum says it is not nice when I am like this. She calls me 'sullen' and nags me to 'cheer up'. But it's not that I am being moody. I just don't always want to join in with the mindless chit-chat when I've got more important things to think about.

I am vaguely aware that the conversation has turned to what we are going to do before the end of the holiday. So far, so boring. Doesn't sound as though I have missed much.

Then Harris suddenly cries out, 'I don't want the holidays to end.' Everyone stops talking and we look at him. His face has collapsed. 'I like us being all together,' he says, throwing himself against Mum and hiding his face in her side.

Mum hugs him to her. 'Little bean,' she says, glancing at Rob questioningly.

Rob gives a tiny nod.

'We have had a lovely time, haven't we?' says Mum. She pushes Harris back into his seat and holds his face in her hands.

'Yes,' says Harris softly. 'I like Finn coming round every day. And I like going to his house too.'

'Yeah, it's been cool,' says Finn.

Yeah, right. So cool. NOT.

'It's been really nice being able to take some time off work. I've loved spending quality time together,' says Rob.

'Yes,' says Mum, her voice a little too high.

Harris jumps up in his chair. 'I LOVE you, Rob and

Finn,' he cries, diving into Rob's lap. He throws his arms around Rob's neck and kisses him hard on the cheek.

Good grief. What a drama queen.

Rob blushes. 'Wow,' he says.

Mum grabs his hand and squeezes it, and Harris snuggles down happily on the bench between the two of them.

Finn looks down at his lap. It's as if he's reading all these actions and knows they mean something. Something I have no idea about.

I glance back at Mum, Rob and Harris. They all have insane smiles on their faces. No one says anything.

OK. This is awkward. Not to mention unsettling. Why do I feel as if I'm about to be told something I don't want to hear?

I take a long drink of my lemonade so that I don't have to look at anyone.

'Maybe this isn't the time . . . I don't know . . . The thing is,' Rob begins, 'Hellie and I have been – talking.' Then he stops.

I put my glass down and see that Mum is chewing her bottom lip and playing with the stem of her wine glass.

'What about?' says Finn, his voice gruff.

My chest is tight. Harris is probably right: I will now burp or get hiccups from gulping the lemonade. I might be having a panic attack, actually.

'And we wanted to talk to *you*.' Mum takes a deep breath, then babbles, 'Aboutusmovingintogether.'

WHAT?

Then I really do burp. Loudly.

'Skye!' Mum exclaims.

'Not quite the reaction I was hoping for,' Rob jokes.

Harris is writhing and gasping with laughter, and the table next to us is joining in. I want to shoot under the table, but I can't. Mind you, Mum has just dropped a bomb so big that under the table might be the safest place to be all round.

I open my mouth to ask Mum to repeat her announcement more slowly, but it's too late. Finn, Harris, Rob and Mum have already started talking all at once. In any case, I seem to have lost the power of speech altogether. I hear the others talking, but it is as if I am watching events through a sheet of glass. It is like one of those nightmares where you can hear and see everyone, but you cannot make yourself seen or heard to anyone else. At least everyone has forgotten about my monster burp.

'YAY! Does this mean we are going to be a real big family?'

'When did you decide this?'

'Finn is going to be my big brother!'

'Darling, stop bouncing. Go back to your seat. There

are a lot of things to discuss.'

'We haven't exactly decided, Finn. We just thought it was time we brought up the subject.'

Eventually I manage to open my mouth and blurt out, 'Well, thanks for the public announcement. And on my birthday, too. How considerate.'

And just like that, the glass shatters and everyone stops talking and turns to look at me.

'Oh, Skye.' Mum looks at me with a pained expression. 'We thought about telling you separately – I was going to say something earlier today – but then we thought it would be better if you were together so that one of you didn't hear it before the other. And we've had such a lovely summer together. Haven't we? We hoped you would be happy. That we could make this evening a double celebration.'

We. We, we, we. WE!

That word used to mean me, Mum and Harris.

Mum leans across the table to try to take one of my hands, but I pull away and sit on them, pressing down hard. I feel so numb inside, I want to make my hands hurt so that I know I am actually really here, hearing all this.

Rob coughs and looks awkward. 'What about you, Finn. What do you think?'

Finn shrugs and the corners of his mouth turn down

in a 'couldn't care less' expression. 'It's cool,' he says. 'I like Hellie. You like Hellie. We all like Hellie. I don't mind if she moves in with us.'

'And me!' says Harris. 'I can come too, can't I? You're not leaving us, are you, Mum?'

Mum laughs, but her eyes are filling up. 'Of course I'm not! And anyway, who said anything about me moving into your house?' she says, to Rob. She is making an effort to keep her voice light, I can tell.

'Well, we're not moving into *yours*!' Finn says. He suddenly sounds a lot less nonchalant.

The numbness in my head melts away: I am starting to feel something now, all right. 'Yeah, well *we're* not moving into *yours*!' I shout, pushing back my chair.

'Skye, sit down,' Mum hisses. 'People are staring at us.'

'They have been staring at us all evening,' I snap. 'Ever since Harris announced to the world that I burp when I drink lemonade and I have Minion underpants.'

'Well, you did burp,' says Harris. 'And you still have the pants. I saw them on the washing line this morning.'

'Shut UP! This is supposed to be my birthday treat!' Oh great, the tears are welling up now. 'I want to go home. I'm going to get the bus.'

'Skye—!'

'Let her go,' Rob says quietly.

I turn to make a dramatic exit – and come face-to-face with a woman who is walking towards us with a huge birthday cake, covered in candles and indoor fireworks. There is a cheer from behind me. The woman beams and says, 'Happy Birthday, Skye!'

And then the whole room explodes into a tuneless rendition of 'Happy Birthday'.

Literally, a roomful of strangers is singing 'Happy Birthday' to me.

Just when I wanted to be at my most invisible.

Not only do I wish it wasn't my birthday.

I wish I had never been born.

Chapter Two

We are silent on the way home. Or at least, Mum, Rob and I are. Finn and Harris are having a tickle fight and thinking of all the words that rhyme with 'bum' and 'poo'. So mature. NOT. If only Aubrey could see Finn like this, she would be mortified that she had ever crushed on him. He is really only an eight-year-old in a fourteen-(nearly fifteen)-year-old's clothes.

Thinking of Aubrey makes me want to talk to her even more than ever. I need to let her know about this cataclysmic announcement of Rob and Mum's as soon as possible. I have literally no one else to confide in. I decide to message her about the whole evening, even though I know she will not be able to reply for hours.

Then, freakily, as I am typing, I get an alert to say that Aubrey has messaged me. I open it and it reads:

Totally awesome! I love it when that happens. ☺

Which is not appropriate at all, seeing as I am in the middle of messaging to tell her about Mum and Rob's totally UN-awesome announcement and the way in which they delivered it. ON MY BIRTHDAY.

Oh, no. Mum is leaning round from the front passenger seat and tapping me on the knee. She is saying, 'Skye, Skye!' in an urgent whisper. What now?

'Skye!'

'Yes?'

'Do you think you could please stop texting and say something?'

'I'm not *texting*,' I say.

'Whatever,' says Mum.

I roll my eyes. I hate it when Mum says 'whatever', like she thinks she is being cool.

'Skye! Please?'

'What?'

Mum frowns and whispers, 'Say something to Rob,' gesturing to him with her head. 'He put a lot of effort into this evening. How was I to know that it was going to be so awful for you to have everyone sing you "Happy Birthday"? You have never minded before.'

I slide down in my seat, fold my arms and stare out of the window. Of course she should have known. And if she thinks that is the *only* thing I have a problem with right now—

'Skye! I am talking to you!'

'Hellie,' Rob says in a low voice.

'No, Rob. I am not going to let her get away with this. You planned a lovely evening, just for her. I can't understand why she is being so sullen.'

Here we go.

'Oh, really?' I snap my head back to face her. 'You can't see what is *wrong* with having a load of strangers stare at you and sing "Happy Birthday"? Couldn't you see they were all laughing? They were probably thinking, "What kind of a freakoid family is *that*!" And we're not even a proper family!'

Mum gasps and puts a hand up to her cheek as though I have slapped her.

I immediately want to take back what I have just said. Mum looks so upset. I open my mouth to say sorry, but she has already turned her back on me. I catch sight of Rob looking at me in the rear-view mirror. He raises his eyebrows. What is *that* supposed to mean?

'Why did you have to say that?' says Harris. 'We were having fun.'

Finn bends forward to give me a sour look, too. 'Yeah, you always have to ruin everyone's fun, don't you, Skye?'

'Boys . . .' says Rob.

Harris sticks his tongue out at me, and Finn turns away and puts his headphones on.

Great. So now I am Public Enemy Number One. On my birthday.

I feel tears roaring up inside me along with a tidal wave of anger. This. Is. Not. My. Fault.

We are turning into our road now. I can't wait to get home. I want to get out of the car right now and hurl myself through our front door and up the stairs and into my room and under my duvet.

While it still is 'our' front door and 'my' room, that is.

I still can't believe Mum and Rob have seriously decided that we should live together. They have obviously made up their minds, so there is no point in trying to talk them out of it. They want to be together. I can't insist on us staying in our house, I know that. This is what I hate about being a child. We are powerless. And yet I don't really want to be a grown-up either. Unless I could jump straight from being like I am now to being a sophisticated grown-up who can run her own life and leave home so I don't have to share it with Finn Parker.

Oh, flip – I don't know what I want, other than for everything to be how it was before our old neighbour Mrs Robertson sold her house to Rob and Finn and moved into a care home. I would give anything – even my signed copy of *Starring Tracy Beaker*, which I won in a writing competition in Year 5 – to go back in time to before this most recent appalling chapter in my mortifying life began.

I seriously hope Mum is not thinking of us moving into Rob's house. He has changed it so much since Mrs Robertson lived there – I hate it. Last time we went round, Rob had ripped out all the bookcases. I couldn't believe that. He is in the building trade and says he is going to 'improve' the house, which in my opinion is a euphemism for 'making a huge mess of everything'.

I wonder where Mrs Robertson's books have gone? She gave me her favourite children's books, but she had so many more that I didn't have room for. I hope she was able to take them with her.

She was the one who got me into reading. I remember her showing me the pictures in her beautiful old copy of *Peter Pan*. The boy who never grew up. (Lucky him.) He said he wanted 'always to be a boy and have fun'. I can't say I want to be a boy, but I wouldn't mind it if I had become frozen in time aged ten. Or eight. I think maybe eight was my favourite age. No one seemed to care who was friends with whom – boys played with girls, and girls played with boys. The only pretending I did was that I could fly or use the *Expelliarmus* charm, whereas now I have to pretend that I *don't* still pretend those things. Which, of course, I do.

I am so deep in these thoughts that I don't notice what has got everyone so animated.

'You are *joking* me,' Rob is saying.

Mum is looking at Rob. Even from this angle I can see that all the colour has drained from her face. 'No,' she whispers.

Finn pulls off his headphones, leans forward to look through the windscreen and says, 'Who's that?'

Harris is craning forward too, which means I can't see anything.

'What's going on?' I ask. I look out of my window, but from here I can't see much.

Rob decelerates and comes to a halt a little bit before his house. I am about to ask why he isn't parking in his usual spot, when I realize it's because there is already someone parked there. It takes a while for my brain to compute what is happening.

The backs of Rob's ears have gone red. 'Stay here a minute,' he says, unbuckling his seatbelt.

No one does what he asks. They are all out of the car in seconds, leaving me to scramble out after them.

'Hey, everyone!' says a voice.

Rob and Finn are walking up the path to their front door.

There, on the step, is a figure I recognize instantly. She is sitting, cross-legged, her face turned up to the setting sun, smiling as though it is the most natural thing in the world to be waiting on someone's front doorstep –

like Gollum does when she wants to be let in and can't be bothered to use the cat flap (which is almost always).

'Hey,' says Finn. He is smiling too, but it is a shaky, uncertain smile. 'Where's the van?' He points at a really cool-looking yellow beaten-up convertible Volkswagen Beetle, with a bunch of stickers clustered on the back window saying things like 'Live, Love, Surf' and 'Totally stoked' and 'Ride the tube to the green room, dude'.

'Is this your car?'

'Uh-huh,' says the woman nodding. She gets up slowly. 'Time to move on, you know?' She yawns and stretches, then standing on tiptoes, she throws her arms wide to envelop her son into a slow, lazy embrace. 'So good to see you, baby,' she croons into his neck.

Harris sniggers – a trick he has learned from Finn. Serves him right.

I am sniggering too: 'baby' doesn't seem very fitting considering Finn is taller than her.

'Yuki,' Rob says. 'We weren't expecting you.' He doesn't exactly sound overjoyed.

Finn's mum – because this, of course, is who it is – pushes Finn out of her hug, keeping one long skinny arm looped around his neck. Her face is dramatic with disappointment. 'What's up?' she says, pouting at Mum. 'Have I come at a bad time?'

Rob gives Mum a look that is hard to read.

Embarrassed? Angry? Sheepish?

Mum kind of shrugs, then starts bustling us all towards our house. 'I think what we need is a nice cup of tea,' she says, as she always does in tricky situations.

Finn looks at me, and I look at him.

This day just got curiouser and curiouser, as Alice in Wonderland might say. At least the attention is now no longer on me.

Chapter Three

I am snuggled up in bed with my cat, Gollum, who is curled on top of my duvet. She likes it when I sit up with my pillows behind me and my legs slightly apart so that there is a dip in the duvet. It is like having a warm, furry, purring hot-water bottle between your knees.

I am supposed to be sleeping. It is pretty late now, but I am finding it hard to relax after what was quite a tense scene in the kitchen, to put it mildly. Also I can hear Rob and Mum's voices - they must still be in the kitchen, which is beneath my room. Although I can't hear what they are saying, the tone is unmistakably stressed.

When we got in with Yuki, Mum tried to get me and Harris to go straight to bed, but it was clear that Finn wasn't going anywhere, so we both dug our heels in and refused to budge.

I actually wish I had come straight up here now, as it was all a bit awkward. Even Pongo wouldn't stop growling, which was bizarre as he is normally over-the-top friendly when Rob and Finn come round.

Rob and Finn were being extremely quiet, though, so maybe Pongo didn't like that. Mind you, Harris was doing enough talking for everyone. He asked loads of questions about why Yuki had come, was she staying, and why didn't she have the van any more. Yuki didn't really answer any of these questions; she merely said things like, 'Life is a journey, sweetie,' and 'You just have to go with the flow.' Mind you, I don't blame her for not answering Harris; he was being pretty irritating. He kept saying, 'Yes, but why?' and 'What does that mean?' over and over.

Meanwhile, Mum was making a huge performance out of boiling the kettle and rummaging for herbal tea, as that is all that Yuki drinks. Mum found this out the last time Yuki turned up unannounced and told Rob off for drinking what she calls 'builder's tea', which apparently interferes with

Yuki's chakras. (I still haven't found out what these are.)

Mum proudly lined up a load of boxes of the most disgusting-sounding drinks, such as Lime and Peppermint Infusion or Summer Fruits with a Hint of Cinnamon. ('Hashtag barf,' as Aubrey might say.) When none of these were met with approval, Yuki said it was OK as she had brought her own green tea with her. (Hashtag double-barf, if you ask me.)

'It's pretty tricky to find it around here,' she told us. 'It has matcha in it.' When we all looked blank, she added, 'I only drink green tea with matcha these days. You should try it, Hellie. It's a great stress reliever. And rejuvenator.'

Rob said, 'Yukiiiii,' in a slow, warning kind of way, and Pongo joined in with an extra-long growl. I don't get what Rob was trying to say. It's not like Yuki had said something insulting. She was only trying to be friendly. Mum is over forty, so she should be interested in tea that makes her look younger. It certainly works for Yuki because she has very smooth skin.

Yuki ignored Rob and got suddenly really over

the top about how wonderful it was that Rob and Mum were 'still together'.

She looked very earnest when she said that. 'It is really extremely cool,' she said. She clasped her hands together to emphasize just how cool it was. I thought that was pretty nice of her, considering she and Rob used to be together. It must be hard for her to see that Rob is with Mum now.

Mum didn't say 'thanks' or react well to Yuki, in my opinion. She just shot Rob a funny, despairing kind of glance, and Rob tried to bustle us all off to bed, saying Finn could camp out in Harris's room tonight, which I thought was odd, as Finn could easily have gone back to his own room.

Yuki clearly thought Rob was being weird. As did I.

'Hey, there's no need to break up the party on my account,' she said. She put her hand on my arm to stop me leaving the room. Then she beamed and asked, 'How old are you, Skye?'

For a second I thought she was some kind of amazing mind-reader, as how would she have known that it was my birthday, but then I realized there were cards on the windowsill and of course I was still holding my presents and the remains of the birthday cake, which I had been forced to try, even though I had been about to run out of the restaurant when it appeared.

I told her I was thirteen and then she did an incredibly generous thing: she counted off thirteen of the tiny skinny silver bangles that she wears and gave them to me.

Rob made a tutting noise when she did that, and Mum went pink.

'What?' Yuki said, her eyes wide. 'I can't sit here and ignore Skye's special day.' She turned to me. 'Thirteen is a very significant age in many cultures,' she said. 'It is the age when you pass into adulthood. A lot of ancient tribes had amazing ceremonies for their kids at that age—'

'Mum,' Finn butted in, 'please don't go into all that. Those stories about people going off into the forest and stuff are freaky and weird.'

Yuki sighed deeply and made a comment about how 'urbanized' Finn had become. I hoped she would go on and tell the stories about the ancient tribes, but instead she went back to saying, yet

again, how 'cosmic' and 'wonderful' it was that
Rob and Mum were 'still together'. This made Rob
tut again.

'Hey, cool it, Rob. I really mean it – no need
to be like that. I just want you to know I love
it that things are working out between you. I
mean, it was all so hasty, wasn't it? You moving
here with Finn, then getting it together with your
next-door neighbour.'

I did think she had a point, but this seemed
to annoy Rob even more. He stared at Yuki with
a level gaze and Mum said nothing, running her
hand through her hair and staring at the floor.

That was when Rob said he was going to take
Yuki next door because he thought she needed to
'relax' (he put a lot of emphasis on that word)
after her long journey, and Mum snapped, 'Fine,
see you later. Or maybe not.' And Finn took
Harris by the hand and said, 'What do you
reckon, buddy – Mario Time?' And Pongo started
barking, and I came up here to hide.

Gollum is purring really loudly now, as though
she is agreeing with me about how odd everyone
is being.

I wish Gollum were my dæmon, like Pantalaimon is to Lyra in Philip Pullman's *The Subtle Knife*, which is the book I am reading at the moment. All the humans in the story have dæmons, which show themselves as animals but are actually part of the human – like their conscience or their inner self. When you are a child, the dæmon can change into different animals. When you grow up, the dæmon fixes as one type of animal. They are very useful, as the humans can ask their opinions on things and also get them to spy, as long as they don't go too far away from the human.

Gollum would make a great dæmon. She already knows exactly how I am thinking and feeling and when to cuddle me and when not to. It also would be amazing to be able to hear what she thinks – and to be able to take her absolutely everywhere with me. It would be especially useful, when I am as confused as I am now, to have a creature on my shoulder who can advise me on what to do – not to mention tell me what Rob and Mum are talking about.

I wonder what Mum's dæmon would be? Probably a parrot, the way she goes on and on - and the way she dresses. Anyway, I am tired now. It's been a weird day and Aubrey has not messaged me in response to my epic rant earlier, so I may as well go to sleep.

Chapter Four

I come down to breakfast the next morning to find
Rob is cooking a full-on fry-up: bacon, sausages, eggs,
pancakes – the works. He is wearing one of Mum's
flowery aprons over an old T-shirt and some tracksuit
bottoms, and he is singing along to the radio with
Harris, occasionally breaking off from flipping pancakes
and stirring eggs to twirl round and use the spatula as a
pretend microphone.

'I'm too HOT – call the po-lice and the fireman!'

'Make a dragon wanna retire, man!' Harris joins in;
then laughs so hard I wouldn't be surprised if his head
literally exploded.

'You could try opening the back door,' I say.

Finn is sitting at the kitchen table, looking at his
phone. He sniggers. 'Good one,' he says, without looking
up.

Harris frowns at me. 'What?'

'If Rob's too hot, he could . . . oh, never mind, it was a joke,' I say, plonking myself down into a chair.

Finn leaps on Harris, making him squeal, and they are off, rocketing out of the room with Pongo snapping at their heels.

Is this what every morning is going to be like from now on? Mornings were hectic enough with just the three of us. I have put up with the mayhem over the summer, but I thought things would go back to normal once we were all back at work and school.

Maybe this is the new normal. In which case, I am not sure I like it.

'Where's Yuki?' I ask. I kind of hope she hasn't gone yet. For as long as she's here, we might be able to delay any more questions about us moving in together.

'Still sleeping,' says Rob, giving a little frown. And then he lifts his finger to his lips.

I look round – does he mean she's sleeping in here?

Rob laughs quietly. 'I meant don't mention her in front of Hellie. Let's just have a nice breakfast on the last day of the holidays.'

Mum comes in as if on cue. She is already fully dressed in one of her more eye-watering numbers. Sometimes I think she should get a job on children's TV instead of her boring office work. She has the kind of boundless, bonkers energy you seem to need to present kids' programmes. She dresses the part too. Today she is wearing a lime-green V-neck sleeveless top, tight white jeans turned up at the ankle, and a white scarf tied around her neck. She has a lime-green flower clip in her hair. At least she is colour-coordinated. That is about all I can say for today's little ensemble.

'Nice look, Mum,' I say. I kind of mean it as an affectionate joke, but it falls very flat.

'Lay the table, Skye,' she says, turning her back on me. No bonkers energy this morning, then.

I look at her sagging shoulders and immediately regret being snippy. There I go again with my head saying one thing and my mouth saying another. I want to tell Mum that I love her and that I am glad she is happy and that Rob is a nice guy and everything, but I also want to explain that I still don't know how I feel about having 'jolly' outings all together like we did last night, and that I am not ready to have to buddy up to Finn like he's my brother. I already have a brother. I am used to being the oldest child – to have Harris looking up to me. (OK, maybe that is wishful thinking.) Ever since Finn turned up, everything has changed. And as for us all living together . . . I just can't get my head around that.

And now Yuki's turned up. It is all too confusing.

I wish I had my own 'subtle knife' so I could slice a door out of thin air and walk through into another world. Seeing as I am stuck here, however, I had better apologize.

'Sorry, Mum,' I mutter, giving her a quick hug as I squeeze past to get the cutlery out of the drawer next to the stove.

I catch her exchanging a look with Rob before she bends to kiss the top of my head. 'It's all right,' she says. 'Let's eat.'

There is a pause and I feel them both looking at me. Then Harris and Finn break the silence by careering back into the kitchen, shrieking and panting. Why do boys do this? They are like overgrown versions of Pongo, who is, of course, right there with them, adding to the racket.

'Requesting permission for Bomber Harris to come into land!' Finn says. He is pinching his nose and talking into his hand, trying to sound as though he is a pilot talking over a radio.

'Neeeeeeaaaaaah!' Harris yells, his arms outspread. 'Is breakfast ready? I'm starvin'!'

'Yes, little bean. Sit down,' says Mum.

'Can't. I'm an aeroplane. Neeeeeeaaaaaah!' He does two laps of the table, Pongo hot on his heels, jumping and yapping.

'Boys!' Rob raises his voice above the cacophony. 'And dog,' he adds, mock-glaring at Pongo. 'Calm down, these plates are hot.'

Harris immediately stops being an aeroplane and lifts his nose to sniff the air. Pongo copies him.

'Wow! That smells AH–MAY–ZING!' Harris throws himself into his chair and picks up his knife and fork. He holds them to attention, his tongue lolling out of his mouth.

'Harris,' Rob says, eyeballing him. 'Be good.'

One of the few great things about having Rob around is that Harris tends to take more notice of him than me or Mum. As does Pongo. Could be the deeper voice, I suppose.

Maybe Pongo is Harris's dæmon. That would make a lot of sense.

All noise and conversation ends as we tuck into huge plates of hot breakfast, all of which I have to admit is delicious. Mum would never make pancakes from scratch. And the eggs are cooked perfectly – no runny bits or overdone dry papery bits, which is how eggs used to be served in this house.

Harris breaks the silence. 'So why has Yuki come back?'

'Harris, not now,' says Mum.

Rob has stopped eating, his fork halfway to his mouth.

'She *is* my mum,' Finn grunts.

'No one is suggesting she shouldn't be here,' Mum says, her voice bright. She gets up from the table. 'More coffee, Rob?'

'I'll get it,' he says, motioning to Mum to stay seated.

'Yeah, but you didn't like it the last time she was here,' Harris says to Finn. 'Does this mean we can't live together now, Mum? What do you think she has done with the van? I liked the van. Maybe she's crashed it. Or sold it to buy some more bracelets . . .'

The last time Yuki turned up unannounced she was driving an awesome campervan decorated with multicoloured swirly patterns and flowers. It turned out that the van had belonged to Rob and Yuki when they were together and that they had planned to take Finn travelling with them. But then Yuki had felt a 'calling' to go and 'pursue her art' in India, and had taken the van with her instead.

Mum lets Harris chatter on and doesn't answer any of his questions. Rob isn't helping either.

I wish they would answer. I want to know a few things too, like: is it good that Yuki has come back? Does this mean, as Harris says, that we won't be moving in with Rob and Finn now? Or will it mean that Finn is round at ours even more so that he can escape his mum, like he did last time when she told him she didn't like him playing the drums?

Whatever the answers are, I can't help feeling that they are not the ones I want.

'Harris, sweetie, why don't you take Pongo around

the block for a little walk after breakfast?' Mum says, in an extremely obvious attempt to change the subject.

It is true that Pongo is being especially bouncy this morning and could probably do with some exercise. He is jumping up beside Mum and trying to pull the bananas out of the fruit bowl. I don't know why he does this as he never eats the bananas, just chews them and then leaves them in a slobbery heap for one of us to slip up on.

'Awww, Mu-um,' Harris whines. 'Can't Skye do it?'

Before I can protest that I am still in my pyjamas and, anyway, Harris never walks the dog, there is the sound of the front door opening and a cry of, 'Hey, guys!' and Yuki walks in.

Mum shoots a look at Rob, which I am pretty sure is secret code for 'You gave her a key?'

'Oh, Rob, not *bacon*?' Yuki says, coming into the kitchen and wagging a finger at him. 'Slipping back into bad habits, naughty boy!'

Finn rolls his eyes. 'Not all of us want to live off lentils and seaweed smoothies, Mum.'

Yuki laughs. 'Not all of us want a heart attack either,' she says.

Mum turns and puts another piece of bacon on Finn's plate. 'Last piece,' she says.

I glare at her. She could have offered it around.

Harris gets up and points at Yuki. 'Why are you here?'

'Don't be rude, little bean,' says Mum. 'And don't point. Can I get you anything, Yuki?' she adds, her voice sugary-sweet.

'I'm fine, thanks, Hellie,' says Yuki, hoisting herself up on to the kitchen worktop and crossing her legs. 'I don't eat breakfast. I need to let my body settle down after my morning yoga session.' She smiles at Harris. 'In answer to your question, angel, I'm here to see my family. Why else would I be here?' she says.

'I am not an angel,' Harris mutters darkly.

The truest thing he has ever said.

'Well,' says Yuki, her smile fading slightly. 'How about I take you all to school tomorrow? That way Hellie could have a bit more time to get ready,' she adds, eyeing Mum's outfit.

I am cringing on Mum's behalf. She looks a mess next to Yuki, who is so fresh-faced it's as though she has just walked out of a crystal-clear waterfall on a tropical island.

'I don't think you could fit them all in that car,' Rob says quietly.

'Yeah, Mum, and it looks like it would break down on the way in any case. You still haven't told us where the van is,' Finn adds.

Yuki tosses her hair. 'Oh Finn, honey, you attach too much importance to possessions,' she says, waving a hand around. Her bangles slide down her arm and tinkle like a wind chime. I look down at my arm and see the ones she gave me yesterday. I touch them, sliding them back and forth, and wonder if I will be able to get away with wearing them to school.

Rob gives a forced smile. 'Some of us have to worry about earthly matters, Yuki. Especially when we have a child to raise.'

'Come on, Harris,' Finn says, getting up suddenly. 'Race you to the trampoline.' Always his solution – to leave the room. (And avoid the washing up, I have noticed.) At least he takes Pongo with them. I go to put my stuff in the dishwasher and pick up the bananas on the way, disposing of them in the bin.

Rob catches my eye and says, 'Skye, would you mind joining the boys? It's just that your mum and I need to have a word with Yuki.' He shuffles over to Mum and puts his arm around her. Mum keeps her eyes fixed on the ground.

'Sure.' I'm not joining the boys. I'll go and get dressed instead. There is no way I want to remain in the room if Mum and Rob are going to start having embarrassing conversations about their relationship.

'Why does Skye have to leave?' Yuki says, pushing herself off the kitchen surface. She comes over and puts her arm around me. We face Mum and Rob like couples about to start some weird kind of old-fashioned dance. 'Surely anything we say impacts on her too? Now that she is thirteen, she has entered the realm of adulthood. She should not be excluded from any conversation.'

I feel myself go red. It is really nice to be treated like a grown-up, but I am getting very strong vibes from Rob and Mum that I am not wanted here. 'I'll go – it's fine.'

I wriggle free from her grasp and run upstairs. Whatever it is that they are about to discuss, I would really rather not be involved.

Chapter Five

I never thought I would say this, but I am actually looking forward to going back to school. Mainly because then I will have Aubrey back, but also because I will be able to get away from my mad household. (This is why I have decided to stay in my room as much as possible until Aubrey comes home.)

I do think it was pretty inconsiderate for my best mate to go away for the WHOLE of the summer holidays. Although, if I were her, I would hardly have kicked up a fuss. I was super-jealous when she told me she was going to New Zealand, as we have only ever gone as far as France. The last holiday we had was camping in Devon. It rained all week. The rain came in through the tent and the colour drained out of the fabric and dyed everything inside it a streaky shade of blue. I had to wear what looked like tie-dyed pants and socks until I grew out of them because Mum said they were still 'perfectly wearable'. (Coming from the woman who thinks it is acceptable to go to the supermarket wearing parrot earrings and feathers in her hair.) That holiday we went canoeing in the rain, cycling in the rain, walking in the rain, and ate a lot of soggy cake (you try keeping food dry inside a leaky tent).

'I don't know why you are so envious,' Aubrey said to me before they left. 'It is winter in New Zealand right now, so it is probably going to rain as much as it did on your camping trip. And don't forget that the only reason we are going is to do the *Lord of the Rings* Tour. I wanted to go in summer and do a zip wire over a valley and go mountain biking and swim with dolphins. But no, my family has to do the Ultimate Tour of Middle-earth.'

Aubrey rolled her eyes when she said this. She rolls her eyes a lot when she talks about her family. I don't know why. Her family is way more cool than mine.

'When are my family going to realize they are living a total fantasy life?' she said. (And what is wrong with living a total fantasy life? I wanted to ask.) 'I have to say I think it is irresponsible of the New Zealand government to allow people to sell "Ultimate Tours of Middle-earth". It is a lie, when you think about it. It just fuels sad people's dreams of meeting a real-life Gandalf. Not to mention encouraging people to speak Elvish, which frankly should be banned.'

I had to bite my lip to stop myself from smiling. I know Aubrey would not want me to remind her of this, but there was a time when she would have killed to be taken on a tour of Middle-earth. I still would, as it happens. I am up for anything that brings a story alive. (Unless it is a film that totally ruins the book by using actors who look nothing like the main characters do in my head, which should actually be a crime.)

I don't know why Aubrey made that comment about speaking Elvish either: we used to pretend we could speak it all the time. If anyone we didn't like came along, we would switch from

English to our own brand of Elvish. The fact that we couldn't understand each other didn't seem to bother us. It was worth it just to see the looks of bafflement on the faces of the other people. The VTs in particular used to get well annoyed with us, but they couldn't prove we were talking gobbledygook as we were so convincing. We even had an accent, which was a cross between Italian and German. It was ace. We frequently had completely hysterical laughter fits while we were doing it, which only made it look more convincing as other people then assumed we were laughing at *them*.

No wonder I don't have any other friends. Aubrey is the only person who has put up with my weirdness all this time.

I literally feel as though my arm has been cut off when she is not around.

Oh, I wish I hadn't written any of this down now. It just makes me miss her even more. I need to talk to her RIGHT THIS MINUTE to try to work out how I feel about Mum and Rob wanting us to move in together.

Thankfully Aubrey is due back this afternoon.

It is school tomorrow, so she has certainly cut it fine. I got a message from her just now, which she must have sent hours ago, before getting on the plane:

> Mum says MUST stay awake when I get home so I get back on UK time! 😖 Am going to have to watch ALL the movies on the plane. Shame that. 😼

At first I was fed up that she hadn't commented on any of the ranty things I had sent her about Mum and Rob. Then I checked my phone and saw that the message had not been sent. Just as well, probably. It was very ranty. I will have to fill her in when she gets here.

Aubrey promised, before she left, that she would race round here as soon as she landed. She said that her parents 'always get mega-grouchy because of jet lag', so she would have to come round to mine to 'get out of the danger zone'.

I literally cannot wait!

But I shall have to, as I still have a few hours to go.

I can't go downstairs though. Now that Yuki is here, I have my own 'danger zone' to avoid. She seems to have a freaky effect on Mum, and Rob gets über-tense when she is around. No, better to stay up here.

Only one thing for it: read. It is always the best way to forget about stressful situations, not to mention the best way to pass the time. Once I am racing towards the Northern Lights with Lyra and Pantalaimon, time will start to speed up - and before I know it, Aubrey will be here . . .

Chapter Six

I have been hiding out in my room all day, lying on my bed. I am about to finish *The Subtle Knife*. I hate it when I come to the end of a book. It's weird to feel like this, really: you read on and on because you want to know what is going to happen, but the feeling of leaving that world behind when you hit the last page is just devastating. It's like you're saying goodbye to your best friends in the knowledge that you are never going to see them again. (This is why I love writing fanfic – it's like being able to stay in touch with those friends, or text them or something! I haven't told Aubrey I still do this. She would think it was lame. She gave it up when she Turned Teen.)

In any case, luckily there is a third book in the series about Lyra's adventures called *The Amber Spyglass*, so I don't have to say goodbye to Lyra yet. I hope it is in the school library. I will ask Mrs Ball as soon as I see her tomorrow.

I am on the last page of the story, savouring each word, when I hear the doorbell go. I know it might be Aubrey, but I have to enjoy almost each last letter.

I have just closed the book with a sigh when Aubrey crashes through the door.

'Skyyyyyyyeeeeeeee!' she shrieks, launching herself on to my bed.

'Aubreeeeeeeey!' I shriek back.

We do our usual thing of screeching and hugging and jumping up and down while hugging and saying, 'I missed yooooou!' over and over again. Lyra might have disappeared for now, but I have something even better: MY BEST FRIEND IS BACK!

'Why did you have to go away for so long?' I say finally. 'It is has been hell with a capital H, spending all summer here without you!'

'It wasn't that long,' she says.

'It was five whole weeks!' I say.

'Yes, but it took nearly two days to get there and two days to get back and for the first two days I was there I didn't know what time it was and kept wanting to sleep during the day, so really I was only actually there for four weeks,' she says.

'You are such a dweeb sometimes,' I say.

'Which must be why we are such good friends,'

she replies, arching one eyebrow.

Aubrey is so cool. I wish I could arch one eyebrow like she does. It is very evil-mastermind-y.

'So come on,' she says. She has gone over to my beanbag and is puffing it up ready to sink deep into its squidgy cosiness. 'What is all the goss?' she says, plonking herself down and wriggling deeper into the beanbag.

'Where do I start? You have NO IDEA how bad it is here,' I say, sitting on the floor in front of her.

'Well I realized that your birthday was not a huge success. I got that complete ESSAY you wrote about the dinner and the cake and everything just before I had to turn my phone off – so I didn't have time to compose a suitably Best Friend-type sympathetic reply.' Aubrey puts her head on one side and does her best to look sympathetic now. 'All those people singing "Happy Birthday" – HASHTAG HIDEOUS! I bet your face was hilarious, though,' she adds, with a wicked eyebrow wiggle. 'Did Finn take a photo—?'

'AubrEEEEEEY!' I protest. 'That was *not* exactly the most important thing that happened that night. I tried to message you again later, but it didn't go through. Oh, flip, it's hashtag DOUBLE hideous. Rob and Mum hijacked the whole thing to announce the most excruciating news—'

Aubrey cuts across me. 'Nothing can be more

excruciating than Dad walking up to a man with a really long beard in "Middle-earth" asking if he was the real Gandalf. He wasn't – surprise, surprise – he was a hiker and didn't take kindly to being confused with a fictional wizard. He gave Dad a long lecture about how irritating it was to be constantly mistaken for Tolkienian characters and how New Zealand had always had men with beards and they had been left to mind their own business until Peter Jackson had come along and ruined everything with his film-making going on all over the place. It was mega-mortifying.' She rolls her eyes and looks to me for a reaction.

I say nothing. Does she *really* think that is the worst thing that can happen to anyone?

'Er, sorry,' says Aubrey, realizing that I look a bit miffed. 'You were saying?'

'Yes, I was,' I say. 'I was talking about the "Big Announcement".' I hook my fingers around the words and put on a stupid announcery-type voice.

Aubrey pulls a face. 'What "Big Announcement"?' she says, copying me. 'The fact that you got a new notebook for your birthday? Or that Harry Potter—where is it, by the way? It sounded lush! Soooo cute of Rob and Finn. Not that I am into Finn any more,' she puts in hastily and immediately blushes. 'I have met someone else, actually.'

I say nothing.

'I met him at the lodge we were staying in,' Aubrey says. 'He has gorgeous blond hair and his eyes are, like, *crystal* blue and when he says "Aubrey" he says it in the cutest way . . .'

Wow. Another crush. Does she literally think of nothing else any more?

She is still talking, oblivious to my total lack of interest in this boy she met. '. . . He's called Zane. How cool is that? He's American and his family are complete *Ring* freaks as well. Luckily he isn't, so I got to hang out with him while our families went to all the talks and film-screenings that were held in the evenings. He is so lush, Skye.' She blushes again and goes all swoony. Her voice has even started to sound American. It is hideously pathetic. 'Do you want to see a photo?'

'Maybe in a minute,' I say hastily. I am desperate to steer the conversation back to my earth-shattering news. 'First I really need to talk to you about Mum's announcement, which kind of ruined my birthday, to be honest—'

'Your birthday!' Aubrey says. She jumps up and rummages in her bag. 'I got you this little present in New Zealand. It is made by the Maoris.' She pulls out a small package with a long, curly-wurly ribbon on the top. 'Zane and I found it while we were shopping on the last day.'

'Thanks! I thought you might have been too busy to get me anything,' I say. I was feeling more than a bit cross that she had already turned the conversation back to her holiday and was not listening to me.

'Too busy to remember my best friend's birthday? You are joking me!' Aubrey says. 'Anyway, it is a big one – THIRTEEN AT LAST!' She squeals and waves her hands.

'Hardly a big one,' I say. 'It doesn't change anything. Not like turning seventeen and being able to drive.'

'Or sixteen and get married!' says Aubrey, making a big deal of fluttering her eyelashes. 'Not that I am thinking of doing that, obviously. Although what with Zane living in the States and me over here, maybe marriage would be the answer.' She takes in my horrified expression and then bursts out giggling. 'Jokes!' she says. 'Oh, boy. Your face! As if I would move away from here and leave my best friend!' she coos in a baby voice.

I give up. I am going to have to find a better time to talk to her about Mum and Rob. She is too hyper right now.

'Come on,' she says. 'Open your present!'

I look down at the little box in my hand. I am being

unfair. She wants me to open a present she chose for me. Of course she doesn't want to listen to me wibble on first.

'Open it, open it!' Aubrey says. 'Come ON!' she says, jiggling on the spot.

'OK, OK!' I pull the ribbon off, then carefully peel back the Sellotape. I always do this with presents, to make the moment last longer.

'OPEN IT!' she shrieks.

I deliberately slow down, but then she lets out a howl of exasperation and lunges at me, making as though to grab the package from me herself.

I swiftly pull off the paper to reveal a small black box. I lift the lid.

'Wow! It's gorgeous!' I say.

Nestling on black satin is a fine silver chain with a beautiful green stone pendant in a twist design. Now I feel seriously bad for getting irritated with her going on about Zane. Not only has she remembered to get me a present, she has chosen an amazing gift.

I lift the necklace out of the box. 'Can you put it on for me?' I ask. I stand up and hand it to Aubrey.

'I'm so glad you like it.' She fixes the necklace on while I hold my hair out of the way. 'We're matching. Look,' she says, pulling a necklace out from under her T-shirt. 'Zane bought me this one when I bought yours. Wasn't that cute of him? The stone is jade – it's a traditional kind of jewellery from New Zealand – and all the patterns mean stuff. They come from Maori art. This twist means "love".' She blushes. 'I don't know if Zane knew that. I mean, I only found out afterwards because someone in the lodge saw me wearing it and told me . . .'

Oh my actual life.

'Anyway, I hope you don't mind,' she goes on. 'I guess for you and me it means "friendship" rather than, like, a romantic thing. I thought, you know, after the whole thing with our friendship bracelets and all that . . . Everything was cool by the end of last term though, wasn't it?' she adds. She has stopped her coy act and actually looks quite anxious. 'The VTs really have learned their lesson about shaming you on social media and . . . I have too.'

I melt inside. Aubrey hates referring back to when we were no longer friends. I don't much like being reminded either, but I won't say that. Her getting me this present is the nicest thing she has done for me in a long while, and I am not going to let anything ruin our reunion today.

'Well I don't care if it does mean "love",' I say. 'I love this necklace, I love the fact that you bought it for me, and I love you too, Aubrey Stevens!'

She throws her arms around me once again. 'Thank you, BFF!' she says.

Because that is what we are: best friends forever. Always have been. We survived all that stuff with the VTs last term, so that proves it, doesn't it? We can survive anything. Even Aubrey's latest crush.

Yes. Everything's going to be all right now Aubrey is back.

Chapter Seven

We have grabbed some snacks from the kitchen, thankfully avoiding having to talk to any of the grown-ups, who have gone next door to Rob's. We are back in my room. Aubrey has shown me all the holiday photos on her phone. Which was kind of unnecessary as I had already seen most of them while she was away because she posted one about every five seconds. Interestingly, she had not posted any of Zane, though. But I have now seen enough images of him on Aubrey's phone to make up for that. A million times over. I also now know his whole life history. In fact, Aubrey has done most of the talking since we got our snacks, and it has been all about Zane. Zane does the best impression of Gollum (the 'real' one, not my cat). Zane looks sooooo hot in skinny jeans. Zane's accent is just too cute. Zane likes peanut butter ice cream. (Hashtag EEUW!) Zane is going to send Aubrey one of his favourite graphic novels.

YAWNSVILLE!

Aubrey is now in the middle of a 'hilarious story' about Zane and his 'amazing' friends and all the 'cool things' they get up to in New York.

I can hardly contain my excitement. NOT.

'And then Zane said—'

'Wow, I am so glad you are back, Aubrey,' I say, loudly.

Aubrey looks surprised, as though I have woken her out of a dream.

'Come here.' I pull her into another brief hug, determined now to move the conversation on. 'It is so good to see you, Aubrey Stevens. What would I do without you?'

And I do mean it when I say that, because I know that, even if she sometimes talks a load of rubbish, I would be a total saddo without her.

'I don't know,' says Aubrey. 'You're making me nervous now. What exactly WOULD you do without me?' She arches her eyebrow again.

I know she means to make me giggle, but I give her the only answer there is. 'I would be sad and lonely and utterly friendless.'

Which is exactly what I was last term when Aubrey went off with the VTs and removed her friendship bracelet, which I had made for her in Year 5.

She did mend it and put it back on again once she realized what an idiot she had been, and we made up. I have to be honest, though – I did always get a twinge whenever I caught sight of it. It never looked the same after it had been broken and tied back on again. I glance down at mine now. It is actually getting a bit manky after four years of wearing it, and it doesn't look that great now that I am wearing the bangles Yuki gave me. I run my fingers over them.

'Don't be a dweeb,' Aubrey is saying. 'You must have hung out with other people while I was away? And you know I don't mind that. Why should I? What *have* you been up to, anyway?' Then she notices Yuki's silver bangles for the first time. 'Hey, those are gorgeous,' she breathes.

'Yeah, Yuki gave them to me for my birthday.' I look up. 'You know what? Now that we have our matching necklaces, I reckon we could ditch our friendship bracelets. What do you think?' I say, turning my wrist over and inspecting the braided threads again.

Aubrey looks shocked. 'Never!' she says. Then she says carelessly, 'Who's Yuki?'

'Finn's mum,' I say.

Aubrey relaxes. 'Oh, right.'

'What, did you think I'd made a new BFF while you were away?' I tease.

Aubrey frowns. 'No, I just—'

'Well, you needn't worry. I was not lying when I said I have had the most boring summer in the history of boringness. Things only got remotely "exciting" yesterday after we got back from the restaurant to find Yuki here. Everything got pretty tense after that. I have been trying to tell you—'

'So, you didn't ever tell me Finn had a mum,' Aubrey says.

'Oh, yeah, you never met her,' I say. I falter as I remember that the last time Yuki came to stay was bang in the middle of the time Aubrey and I were not speaking to each other. 'She came to stay for a bit – it was when you and I weren't . . . well, when we weren't wearing our friendship bracelets.' Aubrey bites her lip. I continue hastily, 'Speaking of Finn's mum, that's part of the whole thing I need to talk to you about—'

'OK, well we are SO not throwing away the friendship bracelets just because *Finn's mum* has given you those,' Aubrey says. She acts like the words 'Finn's mum' have left a bad taste in her mouth. I can't help smiling.

'No, of course not,' I say.

'We promised we would wear them until they fell off, remember? I know I have already broken that promise once, but I am *not* going to break it again, Skye,' she says earnestly. 'Best friends *forever*. And forever means forever, right?' she says. She leans forward and clutches my wrist.

I nod. I make as if to say something, then stop.

'What's up?' asks Aubrey. 'I mean it – I *promise* I will never let you down again. We are OK, aren't we? I know I mucked up big time last term.' She drops my wrist and slumps back into the beanbag.

'Yes, yes, it's not that,' I say. 'It's just when you say "forever" like that – it makes me think, that's all.'

Aubrey peers at me, frowning. 'I don't understand.'

'It's Mum and Rob,' I say. 'Promise you will not tell ANYONE about this?'

'What? Are they having a baby?' Aubrey squeals.

'EEUW! NO! Shut up!' I give her a little push. 'Listen! They want to move in together. Which obviously means we all have to live together. And Rob won't move in with us and I am NOT moving in with them. And it has got me thinking – does this mean we are going to have to move house? Unless now that Yuki's back—'

'NO!' Aubrey cries. She lunges for a hug and grips me so tightly I have to wriggle free or I will stop breathing. 'You can't move,' she says.

'I know! You're squashing me,' I say, in a strangled voice.

She lets me go. 'No, I mean you cannot move *house*,' she says. 'I will not allow it. You won't go, like, miles away from the area, will you?' She looks worried again.

In a funny way, that cheers me up. At least it means she really does care, even if she is not that good at listening. However, in the same instant, I am flooded with worry myself.

'I haven't got as far as thinking about that,' I say. I really haven't: it's only in saying all this stuff out loud to Aubrey that I am beginning to see how scary the future could be. 'I mean, no one's said anything yet about actually really moving. But it seems like we would have to. I mean, our house is pretty full already and, like I say, there is NO WAY I am moving next door. I suppose I thought we might look for another house around here coz of school and Mum's job – and Rob's. But what if they can't afford a bigger house in this area?' I am winding myself up into a bit of a panic.

Aubrey's jaw sets. This is her determined-and-thoughtful face.

'This is just like those problem-page letters you get in *Teen Girl*,' she says. 'I was thinking of writing in to ask about how to handle a long-distance relationship, actually.'

I give Aubrey a look.

Luckily she takes the hint. 'Right, so we were talking about you. Sorry. Why don't we write to *Teen Girl* and get some advice about how to talk to your mum about this? I bet there are loads of comment threads online too about parents who start dating again. Let's get your mum's laptop.'

'No.'

Aubrey frowns. 'Why not? It is always helpful to know that other people are going through the same thing as you.'

'They're *not*, though, are they?' I say, my throat tightening. 'No one is going through exactly the same experience as me. No one knows what it feels like to be me.'

'I know that,' Aubrey says. 'I said the same thing to Zane when we had to say goodbye.' She sighs and has a faraway look in her eyes.

I let my head fall into my hands and then look up at Aubrey with what, I imagine, is a despairing expression.

Aubrey glances back at me. 'OK, OK.' She immediately clicks back into Agony Aunt Mode. 'It wouldn't hurt to see what other people have been through. Would it?'

In the end I agree (mainly to shut Aubrey up, as once she gets an idea in her head it is pretty difficult to get her to change it – she is like Pongo when he has found something disgusting to sniff in the park – she just won't let it alone).

We sneak Mum's laptop out of her room and scuttle back into mine, shutting the door softly behind us.

Within a few clicks Aubrey has found a forum where people are discussing embarrassing parents and their embarrassing relationship problems.

> My dad starting dating a year after my mum died. It makes me angry – like he has forgotten all about her. Am I wrong to feel this way?

> My mum and dad split up when I was really small, but I still hate it that they both have new partners. I hate staying at my dad's because I don't like his girlfriend, and my new stepdad annoys me because he is always telling me off and I don't think he should be allowed to. Mum always takes his side. What should I do?

> My parents are getting divorced and I feel so bad. I just feel that I should be able to stop this happening. They used to love each other, so what has changed? The only thing I can think of is that having kids has made life harder for them – they are always moaning about how much money they have to spend on me and my brother. Is it our fault that they are splitting up?

'Wow,' says Aubrey. 'There are a lot of unhappy people on here.'

'Duh, *yeah*,' I say. 'That would be why it's called a "problem page". Aubrey, this is lame. I don't want to read all this.' I know I am being harsh, but reading these stories – all these real-life unhappy families – makes my stomach churn. Suddenly I don't want to talk about this with Aubrey any more.

'Wait a minute,' Aubrey says, scrolling down the page. 'We haven't read any of the comments or advice yet. Some of this looks good – you might benefit from it.'

Says the girl who thinks she has found true love on the other side of the world, aged thirteen, I think to myself. But I don't say it out loud.

'Listen to this: "My mum recently started dating, and it's really hard to adjust to. I never thought that my mum would meet someone else. I'm happy for my mum, because if she's happy, I'm happy. Make sure that you're comfortable with the person that your mum or dad is dating, and if you're not, talk to your mum or dad about how you feel. It may be awkward, but in the end it's for the best."'

'Yeah, well, I'm really happy for that person,' I say, 'but it is easy to type into a forum that you should "tell your mum how you feel" – it is another matter actually doing it. How can I tell her I am not happy about her wanting to live with Rob when she clearly wants to be with him so much? What kind of a person does that make me?'

Aubrey is still scrolling. 'Hey, what about this? This is specifically about if your mum or dad has died,' she says. 'It could be literally talking about your life!' she adds, beaming.

'Wow. Be brutal about it, why don't you?' I mutter.

But Aubrey is already reading on:

'"It can be really hard to talk to your mum or dad about dating after losing a parent. If you have siblings, they can help relate to what you are feeling about the current situation. If you don't, try talking to a good, trustworthy friend. You just need to realize that your mum or dad is not trying to replace your loved one." Well that's OK, then!' says Aubrey, brightly. 'You have got a good, trustworthy friend.'

'Oh yeah? Who might that be?' I say.

Aubrey looks wounded.

'It's OK, I was only teasing,' I say, but I know I do not sound convincing. This is mainly because even though of course Aubrey is my best friend, she is just making it clearer by the second that she is the wrong person to talk to about this. She doesn't get it. It's another interesting bit of gossip to her. It's not REAL like it is for me.

'Can we stop?' I say. 'I don't want to think about it any more. Let's do something else.'

'I just don't really get what your problem is,' Aubrey says, closing the laptop. 'Rob is super nice, isn't he? And wouldn't it be great to have your mum settled? Maybe she would stop trying out crazy classes and stuff.'

'S'pose,' I say. 'I guess she already has stopped all that – ever since she and Rob got together when she told *me* she was going to a ballroom-dancing class.'

'Well, there you are then,' says Aubrey.

I say nothing. I take hold of the pendant and tilt it to look at it. Are we really best friends again, or is this term going to be just as bad as the last one?

'What's up?' Aubrey asks. 'Have you changed your mind about the necklace? Maybe I should have got you a cat one instead . . . or something from the *Ring* tour. Oh, I've mucked it up, haven't I?'

I look at her carefully. Maybe she really was thinking about me while she was away. Maybe I am overreacting. After all, she is hyper with all her holiday news. And jet-lagged. She might be too tired to deal with all my problems right now.

I give her a strained smile. 'I love it. I really do. Thank you.'

Aubrey squeals. 'And I love *you*!' she says, giving me another hug. 'And I promise I won't be a pain like I was last term, OK?'

'OK,' I say.

70

I just hope she really means it. We have always been fine when it is just the two of us; it's when other people get involved that things get complicated. At least her latest crush lives thousands of miles away. That has to be one less thing to worry about.

Chapter Eight

Rob came round last night after Aubrey left. He said he was leaving Finn to have some 'quality time with his mum'. Harris tried to get himself an invite round to theirs, but Mum insisted he stay with us, so we had an awkward foursome at tea. Rob made his homemade pizza, which Harris loves (I have to say, I do too). While we were demolishing his fantastic Four Seasons, Rob said he had come to talk to us about Yuki.

Mum put on an extra-wide sparkly grin and said, 'You should have brought her round to eat with us.'

And Harris joined in, saying, 'Finn would be here too if Yuki came!'

And he was halfway out of his chair, saying he was going to fetch them, when Rob put a hand on his arm and said, 'It's OK, buddy. They have already eaten.'

Mum said to Harris that Yuki probably didn't eat heavy food like pizza as it would interfere with her cleansing plant-based diet. At that point Rob cleared his throat noisily and said that he knew it wasn't ideal Yuki turning up when she did, but that she had a right to spend time with her son. Mum could hardly argue with that.

Yuki left Rob and Finn ten years ago and has been living on an ashram in India ever since, so Finn doesn't get to see her that regularly. She is the kind of artist who makes those weird structures that people call 'installations', which I must admit I am a bit baffled by. I feel I am missing something, as I really can't understand the concept of putting an old loo seat on a pile of rubbish in the middle of a room in an art gallery and calling it 'The End of Civilization'. I am sure it is due to a lack of a proper education on my part, because people will pay millions of pounds for such things and give out awards and write amazing reviews about them. I should ask Yuki about her art some time. I would love to share some creative tips with a real artist.

Anyway, the evening didn't go very well. The atmosphere was bizarre and tense. Mum didn't talk much, and when she did speak she was snappy. Then she started clearing away our plates before we had finished eating and insisted that Harris and I have yet another early night because of school starting today. At least she and Rob didn't mention us moving house. Maybe they have changed their minds.

I went to bed so early that I have been awake since six writing in my journal with Gollum keeping my feet warm. I suppose I had better get ready. In many ways school might actually turn out to be a less complicated place to be than home right now. At least I will have Aubrey as my right-hand woman again. Time to get going. I just need to get Gollum to move so that I can free my feet. (Easier said than done.)

I go downstairs to find Mum is still in her dressing gown and Harris is feeding Cheerios to Pongo.

'Mum, I thought you said you would take me to school today, seeing as it's the first day of Year 9?' I say.

Mum is drawing a swirly pattern in some spilt sugar. She looks up sleepily. 'Sorry, what?' she says.

I am shocked by how awful she looks. She has dark rings smudged around her eyes, as though she didn't take her make-up off before she went to bed last night, her hair is sticking up like a tangled mass of black wool, and she has way more wrinkles today than I remember her having the last time I looked properly. I hope she has not decided to stop making an effort now that she and Rob are talking about living together. I mean, I am not a huge fan of her dress sense as it is, but even satin and sequins is better than this dragged-through-a-hedge-backwards-in-a-sleeping-bag look.

'Are you OK?' I ask. 'You seem very tired.'

'I'm fine,' Mum says.

'Right – only I have to leave for school in fifteen minutes. You are going to get dressed, aren't you?' I say.

Mum gets up and takes her empty mug to the sink. 'Hmmm,' she says.

'Can I get the bus with Skye?' Harris chirps up.

'No!' I say. And I would say more, except that Rob has just walked in.

He goes up to Mum and puts his arms around her from behind, which makes her shriek and drop her mug. Then she turns around and buries her face in his neck, mumbling something – probably something I don't want to hear.

It is far too mortifying to watch. I wish they would not do this in front of us. Public displays of affection are not appropriate for people as old as they are.

'Well, I am going to have my breakfast in front of the TV,' I announce loudly, and, grabbing some cereal, I leave Mum and Rob to their smooching session.

HASHTAG CRINGE!

'Skye?' Rob calls out after me. 'Be ready in about fifteen minutes. I'm going to take Harris in on my way to work, and Yuki has volunteered to take you and Finn. Let's give your mum a bit of peace and quiet this morning.'

Mum smiles weakly and Harris cheers.

'I LOVE going in your car, Rob!'

At least someone is happy.

I actually feel quite happy myself, once I am on the way to school. It is fun going in with Yuki. The car smells a bit odd and it's got a really noisy engine, but with no Harris to annoy me and Finn sitting in the front, I can spread out on the back seat and enjoy the ride. Beats the bus, any day. Yuki plays interesting music too. It is soothing and no one can sing along to it as it has no words (or none that I can recognize anyway – it is more like humming and funny, throaty umm-ing and aaah-ing). This is a huge bonus as far as I am concerned. Mum and Harris always sing along to whatever is on the radio and it is excruciating, not to mention embarrassing when we stop at traffic lights and people look across and see what they are doing (or even worse, *hear* them if the window is down).

I sit back and close my eyes and let the sounds drift over me. I may as well relax for a bit before the VTs and other horrors of school life come crashing in.

'You like the music, Skye, honey?' Yuki says.

I open my eyes and see she is smiling at me in the rear-view mirror.

'Yeah. What is it?'

'Buddhist chant-y stuff,' Finn grumbles from the front passenger seat.

'Don't be so judgemental, angel,' Yuki says.

Finn grunts and flicks over to the radio and fiddles with the buttons. 'This car is rank, Mum,' he says. 'The radio doesn't even work, the seats have holes in, and it smells. And those surf stickers are way embarrassing. You're too old to have stuff like that. Where did you get this thing?'

Wow. He is being pretty rude. I would have thought he would love his mum driving him to school for once. The car is kind of musty, but it's an OK smell. It makes me think of old buildings – old books too, somehow.

'I would put the roof down, but it's bust. I lit some incense in here this morning,' Yuki is saying, ignoring Finn's grumpiness. 'This car had a difficult journey before I took it on. It needed flushing out – to drive out the bad vibes, you know?'

'No,' says Finn. 'Not really.'

Yuki looks up at the rear-view mirror and rolls her eyes at me, smiling. 'Hope you don't mind it, Skye?' she says. 'Finn has never liked incense. You need to relax, baby,' she says, looking across to Finn. 'You are far too tense for a kid your age. Have you tried that meditation app I told you about?'

'Muuum! Get off my case.'

Yuki laughs. 'Call me by my name, and then maybe I will "get off your case", angel,' she says.

'Stop calling me "angel" and "baby" and maybe I'll relax,' Finn snaps.

I can't help enjoying Finn's discomfort a little bit. He is always the first to side with my mum or Harris if they are bugging me.

'Why don't you like being called "Mum"?' I ask Yuki.

We stop at some lights and Yuki yanks on the handbrake. The car jolts and groans. 'I guess I shouldn't mind so much,' she says. 'My guru said that, actually. He said I had become emotionally constipated and that was why I was blocked in my art – that I had become disconnected with my family and I needed to re-bond.'

'Oh, is that right?' says Finn. 'Who is this *guru*, anyway?'

The lights change and Yuki cranks the creaky old car into gear and revs the engine. 'You know – I told you about him. He is the one who runs things on the ashram. Anyway, he said I was "emotionally and spiritually blocked". I realized after talking to him that I had been a bad wife and mother and that I had abandoned you in pursuit of my art – that I had thought I needed to free myself from the shackles of domesticity so that I could create.'

'Uh-*huh*,' says Finn in a sarcastic tone, nodding long and slow.

'Does that mean that artists need to be free from everyday stuff so that they can think?' I say.

'That's right, Skye! All artists need a creative space so that they can think and let their art breathe,' says Yuki. 'However, I realize now that I took the whole thing way too far.'

'Shame it's taken you ten years to work that out,' Finn mutters.

I decide to ignore Finn's moodiness too. He should be proud of his mum for daring to be so alternative and creative. 'It must be hard, though,' I say to Yuki, 'if you live a normal life and still want to create stuff. I sometimes wish I didn't have to go to school so that I had more time to read and write. There is so much we learn at school that is useless.'

'You *write*?' Yuki cries, flinging her hands in the air.

'Mum!' Finn shouts. 'Keep your hands on the wheel!'

'But that is *awesome*, Skye,' Yuki says with enthusiasm. She does put her hands back on the wheel, but she still says nothing to Finn. I don't blame her. 'You may well find that it is easier to write without the distractions of day-to-day life,' she goes on. 'And I don't have much time for institutionalized education. If it was up to me, Finn would be home-schooled.'

Finn snorts. 'Yeah, well to HOME-school me, you would actually have had to stay AT HOME and not LEAVE,' he says.

'Yes, you're right,' Yuki says sadly. 'That is what my guru said when he said I had taken things too far.' She pauses thoughtfully. 'I see that now. I should have faced up to this and taken responsibility for my actions a long time ago. I have not been fair to you, Finn, honey.' She glances over at him and smiles. 'My art has definitely suffered as a result. But that is all going to change. The time has come for me to be more involved in your life, angel,' she says.

'What do you mean?' Finn asks. There is a note of panic in his voice.

'Well, I thought I would start by asking your head teacher if I could run some mindfulness and meditation classes at your school—'

'NO!' Finn cries.

'Honey, that reaction just proves how much you need to chill. Teens today have so many pressures. You need to learn to find space in your week,' Yuki goes on.

'I think you're right,' I say. 'Life is pretty full-on for us at school.'

Finn turns and glares at me. 'I have *music* to de-stress me, thanks,' he says. He stabs at the button on the ancient tape deck and turns it off. 'And it's way better than your rubbish,' he adds.

We pull up outside school, and Finn is undoing his seatbelt and out of the car before Yuki has come to a full stop.

'Finn, honey!' Yuki protests. But it's too late; he's gone.

She sighs and turns to look at me. 'I worry about the effect of this institution on you all,' she says. 'The bells rings and you all rush off. You're like animals in a laboratory. What would happen if you just skipped class for once?'

'I – I guess I'd get detention,' I say.

'Skye, Skye,' Yuki says sorrowfully. She reaches back round and touches my hand. 'If you want to be a writer, you're going to have to learn to break the rules a bit – go against the tide, you know? You can't think like everyone else if you want to be truly creative, take it from me.' She touches the bangles she gave me. 'Good to see you're still wearing these. I am guessing that breaks a school rule?' She winks.

'Er, probably. Thanks for the lift,' I say, undoing my seatbelt.

'I know what you're going through, hun,' Yuki says. The seriousness in her face makes me stop. I hope she's not about to try and talk to me about Rob and Mum. 'It's hard for you, right?'

I nod, not daring to say anything.

'It's not cool, trying to create in isolation – in an environment where people don't understand your artistic needs,' she says.

Phew. Not a big heart-to-heart about family then.

'Yeah, I s'pose,' I say. I gather my stuff and open the door.

'Have a good day, honey! See you later.' Yuki puts the car back into gear, ready to move off.

As I watch her go, I am struck by how Yuki seems to get how important writing is to me. More than Mum ever has. I don't think Mum even knows I want to be a writer. She is too wrapped up in her own life to care. And Aubrey – well, she and I used to love writing fanfic together, until Aubrey decided it was 'for little kids'. We had a major Harry Potter and Twilight phase, and loved making up stories based around those characters. I still go on those sites, but I haven't dared mention it to Aubrey since she dissed it. Mrs Ball has encouraged me, but she is not an artist herself. She doesn't talk like Yuki does about 'breaking the rules' and 'being truly creative'.

Does this mean I need someone who understands me better?

Could that someone be Yuki?

Chapter Nine

I am still thinking about this as I make my way to the locker area. I am not sure I want to go as far as showing Yuki anything I have written – my journal is private stuff about me and my family, and I'm not sure she'd really get the fanfic stuff. However, I can feel a warmth spreading through me as I replay those encouraging words again: '*If you want to be a writer, you're going to have to learn to break the rules a bit – go against the tide . . .*'

My phone beeps and I take it out of my pocket. Oh no! Aubrey has been texting me the whole way in. There is a stream of them on my phone. I read them quickly, feeling guilty:

Why R U not on the bus? 😵

Are you coming in with Fit Boy Finn this morning? 😊

> Tell him I have missed him! 😺

> DON'T! Don't tell him that. Didn't mean it!!! 😦

> U haven't told him, have U? 😖 😖 😖

> If U have, tell him I am already spoken for . . . ♥ 😺

So. Turns out I didn't need to feel guilty at all. There was I thinking Aubrey might be desperate to see me, but looks like it's going to be all about boys again this term. I spot her waiting by the Year 9 lockers, the VTs hovering nearby. Has she been gossiping with them already? Telling them about her amazing trip to New Zealand and her holiday romance? That will get her in with the popular crowd immediately. She wouldn't have told them about Rob and Mum, would she? I feel a bit sick as I think of what that would do to me: the VTs and their hangers-on making jokes about my mum snogging Finn's dad. Argh! I can't bear to think about it.

Aubrey is looking left and right, scanning the crowds as people ebb and flow around her. Is she looking for me or Finn? I am not sure I want to be an extra in The Aubrey Show. I decide to go straight to the library instead. Maybe the library is 'the creative space' I need where I can 'think and let my art breathe'.

Too late, Aubrey has seen me. Her eyes light up and she runs towards me, arms open for a hug.

As she reaches me, lots of things happen at once.

Finn walks by with two of his friends from his band, the Electric Warthogs.

Aubrey stops in mid-run and calls his name.

Finn swerves to avoid us.

Aubrey turns back to me, blushing.

A boy carrying a musical instrument case walks between us.

Aubrey throws her arms wide again to hug me and the boy gets caught in the crossfire, his case thwacking against my legs.

'Hey!' I yell. I act automatically, shoving the boy and Aubrey away so that they stumble backwards against the lockers, clinging on to one another and shouting.

The VTs have seen the whole thing, as has Finn – and everyone else in the area. I do feel bad for pushing them so hard, especially since the instrument case springs open and an expensive-looking electric guitar falls out.

But seriously! How embarrassing can you get? A group hug with a boy – *and* one I don't even know – that equals Mortification Level at *least* one billion!

Gales of mocking laughter swirl around me as Aubrey and the boy disentangle themselves. I literally do not know where to look.

The boy is checking the guitar, plucking gently at the strings, looking it over for damage.

'Great new way to get a boyfriend, Aubrey!' says Izzy Vorderman, shooting me a snidey look.

'Not the best way to "catch" a man, is it?' says Livvy, the other half of the VTs.

'Actually, I already have a boyfriend,' says Aubrey.

'Ooooo–OOOOO–ooooo!' the twins crow in unison. 'Get you!'

I immediately feel sorry for Aubrey and urge my brain to come up with a snappy comeback to the VTs. As usual, however, my brain does not oblige. The VTs snigger, as they strike a pose with their hands on their hips, faces set in mockery.

Luckily everyone's attention is focused on the boy. Finn is helping him with his guitar. 'You OK, mate?' he says.

'Yes, I think so,' says the boy. His voice is deep and musical. I wonder if he sings as well as plays.

Where did that thought come from at a time like this?

'Don't pay any attention to Twin Freaks over there,' Finn is saying. 'They never have a nice word to say about anyone.'

The small crowd around us laughs. Izzy and Livvy visibly deflate, their shiny-faced sarcasm evaporating.

They slouch off to their lockers and begin throwing stuff in, muttering to one another. Now there is nothing more to see, the crowd also starts to disperse to class.

The boy smiles shyly. 'Thank you,' he says to Finn. 'I don't think anyone meant to be unkind.'

Finn snorts. 'You reckon? You must be new if you aren't aware of the VTs' little routines.'

'I am,' the boy says. 'My name is Effi Afolayan. My family moved here this summer.'

He sounds very formal: he speaks in a much more grown-up way than any of the rest of us. I can't help noticing his eyes. They are so dark and shiny. Like smooth black pebbles. He looks right at me suddenly and grins, showing the brightest, cleanest teeth I have ever seen on anyone in real life. They are Hollywood white. I try to smile back, but only manage a weird kind of teeth-baring grimace, as though I am trying to show him how rubbish my own teeth look in comparison. *What am I like?* I feel as though everyone must be able to read my mind.

Thankfully Finn and his friends are more interested in the guitar, and Aubrey is more interested in gawping at Finn and his Hog mates, who are waiting for him – she is such a freaking groupie. I try to avoid looking directly at anyone. I am willing the bell to go so that I can have an excuse to leave the scene.

'So, you play bass?' Finn is saying. 'You should come along to band practice. We need a new bass this year, don't we guys—?'

'Angel!' a familiar voice rings out. 'Angel – you forgot your falafels.'

I turn to see Yuki, who is running towards us, waving a brown paper bag in the air. I am impressed. If I leave something in the car or at home, Mum says it is tough, and then gives me a lecture on how she is not a taxi service.

Finn does not seem to realize how kind his mum is, though. His expression is thunderous. Mind you, his mates are now laughing at him, and parroting 'Angel!' in a sing-song voice. I have to admit that it is rather funny.

'Mum, you can't just walk in here,' he says, scowling.

Yuki is not fazed. 'It's OK, honey. I went to the school office and they said you'd still be by the lockers as the second bell hasn't gone yet. I didn't want you to forget your snack. I don't want to *think* about the processed rubbish they feed you here in the canteen.'

The Hogs are loving this. They have backed away and are standing to the side of the lockers, whispering behind their hands and giggling.

'Yeah, well, you have to go now, Mum,' Finn says.

'OK, chill babe,' she says. Then she holds her hands up to her face in prayer, bows her head and says, 'Peace.'

And with that, she turns to go.

'Wow, peace, man,' says one of the Hogs.

'Yeah, peace, *angel*,' adds his mate.

Finn sets his jaw and storms off to class.

The bell does ring then, putting a stop to any more excitement. Aubrey and I quickly throw stuff in our lockers and head off to our new classroom.

I feel someone tap me on the shoulder. It is Effi.

'I will see you later,' he says, his dark eyes holding my gaze.

'Yes,' says Aubrey. 'See you at lunch.'

I clear my throat to speak, but nothing happens. I appear to have lost my voice.

Effi's smile fades. 'I hope so,' he says.

I find myself thinking: *I hope so too*.

Where did that come from?

Chapter Ten

I am walking in to lunch with Aubrey and wondering whether I should try talking to her about the muddling thoughts I am having. I have not been able to concentrate all morning. I am either thinking about what Yuki said about my writing or I am thinking about Mum and Rob saying we should move our families in together or I am thinking about a pair of shining dark eyes and a dazzling smile—

EMBARRASSING THOUGHT ALERT!

I don't even know how to begin to talk to Aubrey about all this, which is just so weird as I normally have no problem taking to Aubrey about anything (when I can get a word in, that is). Mum says she can't understand what we have left to talk *about*. She says we have known each other so long and see each other so often, we must have exhausted all possible topics of conversation by now. Which just goes to show she has totally forgotten what it is like to be our age. And also proves that it must be boring being grown-up if you really do run out of things to say to your BFF.

Aubrey is doing enough talking for the both of us, anyway, so she hasn't noticed that I am being quiet and thoughtful.

'So, do you reckon that new boy will join the Hogs? That guitar looked pretty special. Expensive too. What was his name? Enni? Ellie? No, that's a girl's name. I *love* his voice – it's kind of – I don't know – melodious, don't you think? Where do you reckon he's moved from?' She stops to draw breath.

'I – I don't know,' I say.

'He's almost cute enough to stop me thinking about Zane. JOKES! I am NEVER going to stop thinking about Zane. Did I tell you he messaged me last night? It is sooooooo annoying him being in a different time zone. Aaaaaanyway,' she says, pausing to breathe again, 'tell me what's Finn's mum like?'

Wow, OK. Talk about a curveball change of subject. Not that I am *not* relieved to hear her stop talking about Zany Zane.

'Yuki? She's nice,' I say. 'She's an artist. Conceptual stuff, you know,' I say, keeping it vague. I couldn't begin to explain to Aubrey what Yuki really does. 'I haven't seen any of her work yet, but it's like über-modern, apparently. And she's kind of a free spirit – into meditation and yoga and stuff. She's pretty different from anyone else we know,' I say.

'Sounds cool,' Aubrey says.

She is looking at her phone. Great. Checking for messages from The American, no doubt. I don't know if I am going to be able to handle this crush. I need her mind to be here, in the present, next to me – not floating off across the Atlantic, dreaming about her heart-throb hero. She hasn't asked me anything about Mum and Rob since we looked at those problem pages yesterday. Maybe she thinks I am 'over it' and that reading a few lame online forums was enough to sort my head out. I decide to bring up the subject to see what her reaction is. Or to see if she is even listening to me.

'Yeah. So, about Mum and Rob. What do you think?'

'I don't know, Skye. Just say how you feel,' she says vaguely.

'I can't.' I wait to see if she looks up. No chance. 'I don't have those kinds of cosy heart-to-hearts with Mum. It's just not me. The thing is—'

Aubrey realizes the queue is moving on and stuffs her phone into her pocket, turning abruptly to start heaping salad into a bowl.

'Aubrey, please listen to me. I need to talk to you about this!' I say.

Aubrey looks up at me. 'You are,' she says, puzzled.

'But are you listening?'

'Yes. What do you think tuna is like with carrot salad?'

What is the point? I might as well be invisible. I turn away from her and start filling a glass with water.

'Hi,' says a deep voice. 'Can I please sit with you?'

I turn round a bit too suddenly and my hand glances off Aubrey's shoulder. Unfortunately it was holding the water glass I have just filled. The glass tips back and crashes to the floor, and the water falls all down the front of the new boy.

'I'm sorry! I'm sorry!' I shriek and step back on to Aubrey, who drops a tuna-filled spoon to the floor with a clatter. Blobs of tuna splatter her legs. 'You idiot!' she cries.

Effi's smile has disappeared and turned into a round 'O' of shock.

'I'm sorry!' I say again, grabbing a handful of paper napkins from next to the salad bar. Before I can stop to think about what I am doing, I start rubbing the front of his shirt with them.

He puts his hands on mine and gently lifts them away. 'It is fine,' he says quietly. 'It is only water. It will dry.'

Aubrey giggles. The sound of the glass smashing and the spoon falling on the hard lino floor has already caught the attention of a lot of people in the dining room, so now I have a lovely audience ready to appreciate the sight of me rubbing Effi's chest with a wad of soggy paper napkins.

'Interesting, the way you two keep *bumping into* the new boy,' hisses Livvy Vorderman as she slithers by to the hot-meal counter.

Effi turns to her and says, 'It was an accident. Please do not make Skye feel bad.'

He knows my name, I think. *How does he know my name?*

Livvy is looking pretty miffed that her nasty little comment has backfired. 'Oh, nothing is an accident where Skye is concerned,' she snaps back. 'She and her little friend are so desperate to get a boyfriend, they'll do anything.' She puts her hand on her hip and looks triumphant.

'I've already told you,' Aubrey begins, but she is interrupted by a voice behind us.

'What would *you* know about boyfriends?'

Livvy's jaw drops.

I look round. It's Finn. 'Careful the wind doesn't change, Livvy,' he says. 'You might stay like that, and then *you* will *never* get a boyfriend. And you certainly won't win any more beauty competitions,' he adds, making a reference to the hilarious Baby Beauty Contest photos that he found online last term when the VTs were bullying me.

Livvy opens and closes her mouth a couple of times, and then turns to go. It is clear Finn has won this little contest – game, set and match.

'Come on, guys,' Finn says. 'Let's go and find somewhere to sit. Effi?' he calls over. 'OK if we join you?'

I am not sure I want to go and sit next to the boy I have collided with twice in one morning. But he is new. And I tell myself he probably feels like a loser having had two accidents on his first day. It will make him feel better if we sit with him.

'Way to go, Finn!' Aubrey says. Then she leans in and nudges me in the ribs, whispering, 'Maybe it's not so bad to have a big-brother figure stick up for you every once in a while!'

I want to shout that he is NOT my brother.

But, thinking about it, maybe she is right about having Finn there to watch my back.

'Yeah, I s'pose he didn't have to stick up for us like that,' I mutter.

Oh flip! I think sometimes it was easier when I didn't like Finn at all. At least then I knew where I was. I am just SO CONFUSED about everything.

Chapter Eleven

One person who definitely is NOT confused about how they feel about Finn is Harris. Harris thinks Finn is the bee's knees. And the sparrow's kneecaps. And the elephant's pyjamas. In other words: Finn is GREAT in Harris's world.

But then, to be fair, Finn did an amazing thing for Harris last term. He stuck up for him when he was being seriously bullied, and actually stopped the bullying altogether.

Mind you, Harris does not help himself, in my opinion. The reason he was being bullied was that he had joined a dance class at school. He thought he could enter a ballroom-dancing competition with Mum, so he went for lessons to get extra practice. Not only was he the only boy in the class, but he had also dressed in some pretty outrageous outfits, based mainly on things he had found in Mum's wardrobe - never a good place to go looking for inspiration, unless you want to look like something the cat has dragged in from the local recycling bin. It would be bad enough if Mum's dress sense were that of a normal mum, but because she loves all things sparkly, velvety, satiny and anything with feathers, Harris inevitably ends up looking like an overdressed vintage Christmas tree whenever he tries on something of Mum's.

I would have thought he would have learned his lesson about doing things that make him stick out from the crowd (like wearing a feather boa and dancing the tango), but it turns out he has even bigger ideas this term.

He came in this evening, completely overexcited - or even more overexcited than usual, should I say - because his school are putting on a Christmas performance of *The Wizard of Oz*. They are auditioning at the start of term because there are going to be weekly rehearsals from now until the performance. Now that Harris is in Year 5, and therefore almost at the top of the school, he reckons he stands a good chance of getting a big part.

The only problem is, he is not going to be content with any of the obvious roles. Not the Tin Man or the Lion or the Scarecrow for my brother. Not even the title role of the wonderful Wizard himself. Oh no.

Harris wants to be Dorothy.

He literally could not stop whirling and twirling when he told us.

'I have got it all worked out!' he said. 'I can borrow your gorgeous sparkly red shoes, Mum, and I can take Pongo along to be Toto! Toto even sounds a bit like Pongo, so he won't get confused when he is training for the role.'

Harris then proceeded to demonstrate by crying, 'Toto! Toto!' at Pongo while holding a dog biscuit in the air.

Of course the stupid dog sat up and begged.

I pointed out that you could call Pongo 'Wheelie Bin' or 'Idiot Face' and he would do anything you wanted as long as there was a biscuit in it for him.

Mum, of course, thought the whole thing was a 'splendid idea' and wanted to know all about it.

'When are the auditions?' she asked. 'I think

we should practise. You need to get into your character. Let's get the film and watch it tonight.'

I then tried pointing out that encouraging Harris to dress up and go up on stage with our mentally challenged Labrador might just possibly be asking for trouble.

'Pongo will spend the entire time eating inappropriate things and throwing them up,' I said. 'And if you think people thought your dancing was weird last term, Harris, how are you going to cope with everyone calling you "Dorothy" for the rest of your life?'

But my wise words fell on deaf ears, as they always do.

Mum got irritable and told me off for 'not being very supportive'. She said she thought it was 'wonderful that our little bean wants to express himself in a feminine role'.

I tried explaining patiently that I only had my brother's best interests at heart, but they ignored me as usual, and I was told to stop being negative and even to 'get a life'.

'No one says that any more!' I railed at Mum. I hate it when she tries to sound young.

She is always saying things she thinks are cool when they are SO not. Particularly when they come out of her mouth.

Mum then got über-huffy with me and said I needed to be less critical and have more respect for her and that I should support my brother and realize that I wasn't the only one with dreams. Then she stormed out of the kitchen, which is something I am never allowed to do when she is talking to me. 'Hashtag double standards,' as Aubrey might say.

So much for 'talking to my mum and telling her how I feel about things'. If she is going to be *this* touchy about me expressing an opinion on the language she uses – and if she can't see that I am only trying to HELP Harris so he doesn't get bullied again – then how I am going to tell her how I feel about Rob becoming my new dad? It all seems pretty clear to me: Mum just hasn't got time for me any more.

I have left Harris and Mum curled up on the sofa with Pongo, watching the film of *The Wizard of Oz* and singing along tunelessly. Pongo has just started howling. I strongly suspect he is trying to tell them something, but they probably think he is singing along as well. Gollum is under my duvet. If she could stick her paws in her ears, I think she would. I am going to have to listen to an audiobook with my headphones on. I cannot stand the voice of the Wicked Witch of the West. It has penetrated my brain so that it feels as though someone is driving a rusty nail through it. Someone should have told the actor to hold back on the cackling. It can get pretty wearing after a while.

At least Harris's announcement prevented Mum from calling a family meeting to discuss us moving. I know the idea is not off the agenda, because she has been looking at houses online and has sent off for a load of estate agents' details already.

What can I do to prevent us leaving this place? I wish Aubrey wasn't so obsessed with Zane. I can't get her to focus on my problems for more than five seconds before she is sighing and looking all lovesick. I made the mistake of texting to say that at least my problem was a real one that needed a real solution, whereas hers was a total fantasy that was never going to become a reality.

She has not answered any of my texts since I said that.

The only thing that would stop me having to move is if I got a letter through the window right now informing me that I have got a place at Hogwarts. I have often thought how cool that would be.

Even facing Snape or a whole pack of Dementors would be better than living with Rob and Finn.

But then I think about how much Mum and Harris want it, and how, as Aubrey says, Finn did step in with the VTs the other day . . .

ARGH! I just have such a jumbled mix of emotions and thoughts going round and round in my head. Mrs Ball always says it is a good idea to write things down to get a sense of how you feel, so here goes (I am just going to list the first things that come to mind):

1. I really like Rob, and I like that he makes Mum happy.
2. I don't want Rob as my dad.

3. I can't remember my own dad and that makes me sad.
4. I am cross that Mum seems not to be sad about Dad dying any more.
5. I am happy that Harris likes Rob and also (secretly) I am happy that he gets on with Finn, because I can see they have fun together.
6. I hate the fact that Finn can make my brother laugh more than I can.
7. I liked how it was with Finn at school today.
8. I don't want to move house.
9. I can't see how we can all fit in here.
10. I don't want to move next door and watch new people move into our house.
11. But I like Rob and I like that he makes Mum happy . . .

OK, so that wasn't much use. On and on and round and round the thoughts go until I feel dizzy and sick from trying to think it all through.

Like Dorothy inside the twister in Kansas.

If only the Good Witch of the North could

come and give me some advice. Maybe Aubrey is right and I should write to an agony-aunt-type person. But I don't want to write to a stranger who doesn't know anything about me and my family.

Mrs Robertson would know what to say. I miss her so much. I used to go round when she lived next door and talk about everything and anything. Not that I had problems, exactly, when I was younger. I could be just chatting to her about a book that she had lent me, and then, before I knew it, I would be talking to her about something that had happened at school that day, and she would be listening and offering me biscuits along with some excellent advice.

Like the time we had to dress up for Red Nose Day at school and Aubrey insisted we dress from top to toe in red, which meant we also had to spray our hair red, apparently. Aubrey went to the pound shop and bought two cans of coloured hairspray. She made me promise I would do it just before leaving the house, and because we knew our mums wouldn't let us colour our hair, even with wash-in/wash-out spray, we made a plan to wear bobble hats pulled down over the top.

Well, just my luck, the can that Aubrey had given me was out of date. (I guess that's what comes from buying things from the pound shop.) And so by the time I got to school, the dye had had a rather unfortunate effect on my hair.

It had gone green.

So you can imagine the comments that day, what with my surname being 'Green'.

Let's just say it was not a good day.

It was made even worse by the fact that I couldn't get home quickly to wash it out because Mum was working late that evening.

So I went round to Mrs Robertson, who often looked after us when Mum was late, and sobbed my heart out to her.

And that is the day she lent me her copy of *Anne of Green Gables*, turning straight to the chapter where Anne dyes *her* hair green by accident too! (Nothing to do with the 'gables' of the title - that is where she lives.) Mrs R then helped me to wash my hair in her kitchen sink, rubbing my hair with baking soda first, and putting a shower cap on it so that I could leave it in for a bit. Then she washed my hair twice and put some yummy strawberry-scented conditioner on it, and hey presto! The green had faded away. There were still traces of it, but she told me to take the baking soda and use it again that night and the next morning, and she was right – I went to school looking perfectly normal (or as normal as I ever look) the next day.

Plus I got the copy of *Anne of Green Gables* out of the whole episode. So, to be honest, it was almost worth going through the trauma of spending all day sweating under a bobble hat with green hair.

Anne Shirley, the main character, is a character from a book with whom I feel I have a lot in common. She too wants to be a writer and also, at times, feels very alone in the world. She is an orphan and gets sent to live with a couple of old childless people who are brother and sister. The sister is quite mean at first and doesn't like Anne, because she wanted to adopt a boy instead of a girl – but the brother loves Anne straight away, and they become 'kindred spirits'.

Sometimes I think that Mrs Robertson was my kindred spirit.

I know that sounds as though I am being unfair towards Mum. I mean, I am not a complete orphan like Anne. (Although the dictionary definition of an orphan is actually someone who has lost one *or* two parents, but no one ever seems to use it that way.) There are times, though, when I do feel alone - especially now that Mum and Harris are so happy, and Aubrey is wrapped up in her overseas romance and doesn't really get what I am going through.

Remembering this has made me realize something . . .

It is obvious, isn't it? I should go and see Mrs Robertson! She would be the best 'trustworthy friend' with whom to talk this all through.

I remember Mum mentioning the other day that she had spoken to her on the phone and that she was well enough to have visitors now.

Maybe Mrs Ball is right - writing things down can help me to work things out, even if it only takes me one step further on rather than solving all my problems at once.

Chapter Twelve

The next day, after school, I ask Mum if I can go and see Mrs Robertson.

'Skye, it's not a good time,' Mum says. 'We are having a family meeting about the move – you know that.'

Great. Looks as though The Wizard of Oz *distraction didn't last long enough.*

I try a different way of getting Mum off track.

'Can Aubrey come for tea?' I ask. 'You always say she is one of the family.'

Mum lets out an irritable sigh. 'You have just spent all day together. Surely she needs to get some early nights in to make up for the jet lag? She must be exhausted going straight into a new term after that long flight.'

'No, I don't think she's really struggling with that—'

'Skye!' Mum snaps. 'No, OK? We need to talk to you all, and if Aubrey comes round you'll only disappear to your room. I need your full participation this evening. In any case, Yuki is coming too, so there won't be enough food, let alone enough space around the table for any more people.'

'How come Yuki gets to eat with us and not Aubrey?' Harris chips in. 'Yuki is not in our family either.'

'WHAT are you wearing?' I ask.

My brother has a blue ribbon in his hair and has on what looks like one of Mum's blouses and a blue-and-white checked apron. The outfit is finished off with the red sparkly shoes he was talking about the other day. And he is sitting in Pongo's bed – with Pongo.

'This is going to be my outfit for the audition,' he says, smoothing down his 'skirt'. 'Pongo – I mean, Toto – and I are bonding and getting into character.'

'Does everyone have to "bond" around here?' I ask. 'Harris is "bonding" with Pongo; Mum wants us to "bond" with Rob and Finn; Yuki needs to "re-bond" with her family—'

'OK, Skye, that will do,' Mum interrupts.

'I don't want Yuki to bond with anyone,' Harris grumbles. 'And I *really* don't want her to have tea with us.'

'Don't be rude, little bean,' Mum says.

'Yuki *is* Finn's mum,' I point out. 'Although it might be a problem her having tea with us. She doesn't eat meat, does she?' I am eyeing the ingredients in the recipe for lasagne that Mum is laying out on the kitchen work top.

Mum sighs again. 'Noooo,' she says. 'But she has *kindly* agreed to eat the vegetables I am cooking to go with it. Apparently she doesn't want me to go to any trouble to cook a special meal for her. Which is – nice,' Mum adds. She pulls a funny face when she says this, as though she doesn't think it is 'nice' at all.

I don't get Mum's problem. If Yuki is not even going to eat half the food, Aubrey could easily have come for tea . . . Still, it is not worth arguing with Mum once she has got herself into one of her snappy and illogical moods. I decide to keep quiet and lay the table instead in the hope that might cheer Mum up.

There is the sound of the front door closing, and a few seconds later Rob and Finn come into the kitchen. Rob has brought a bottle of sparkling wine and Finn is holding a tray, which is releasing a rather strange aroma – a bit like cooked mud. Or how I imagine cooked mud might smell. I wrinkle my nose. Harris pulls a face. Mum coughs and turns away.

'Brownies,' he says in answer to our reactions. 'Vegan – Mum made them.'

'YAAY!' Harris shouts, 'I LOVE brownies.' He leaps out of Pongo's bed and hugs Finn around the knees. Pongo leaps out too and rushes at Finn.

'Whoaa! Careful, guys!' Finn laughs. 'Trust me, Harris. These are not your average brownies.'

Mum lifts the foil that is covering the tray. 'So we can see – and smell,' she mutters. Which I think is very rude of her.

Luckily no one else seems to hear her above Harris's rumpus.

'Come here, you!' Finn puts the tray of brownies on the counter top and charges at Harris, who squeals happily and allows himself to be turned upside down (which is unfortunate, as I get an alarming view of my brother's Super Mario pants). Then Finn flings him over his shoulder and goes running with him out into the hall, Pongo following.

'What's with the dress, buddy?' I hear Finn shouting.

'I'm going to be Dorothy!' Harris replies.

'Awesome!' shouts Finn.

Rob raises his eyebrows and opens his mouth to comment.

'Don't,' I warn him.

'Those brownies look – original,' says Mum.

'I know, even the dog isn't hanging around for one,' Rob jokes.

Mum curls her lip.

'What's the problem?' I say. 'You're always saying we should try new things.'

'Yeah,' says Rob, looking at Mum. She avoids his gaze and picks up an onion, inspecting it closely. 'So good to see them getting along,' Rob adds, nodding out the door after the boys. Then he catches my eye and looks guilty. 'Sorry if Finn and Harris leave you out sometimes,' he says.

'It's fine,' I say. 'Finn is welcome to hearing "Somewhere Over the Rainbow" a million and one times before tea.'

Rob grins. 'Yes, I can see how that would get irritating.'

It's the kind of thing you'll have to get used to if we all move in together, I think. But I don't say it. He looks so happy. Especially when he looks at Mum.

Here I go, getting all confused again . . .

'What's the sparkling wine for?' Mum says. 'We haven't got anything to celebrate yet.'

'Oh, I don't know – I reckon our two families coming together is a pretty good cause for celebration,' Rob says, putting his arm around Mum's waist and kissing her on the cheek.

Urgh! PDA Alert!

Quick, think of something to say before they start actually snogging.

'Where's Yuki?' I ask.

Mum wriggles away from Rob and turns to start

chopping a red pepper. She attacks it with great enthusiasm. I don't think I have ever seen her enjoy preparing vegetables so much before.

Rob looks at Mum, biting his lip. Then he says, 'Yuki's having a shower. She'll be over in a minute. Maybe we should take a look at those brochures before she gets here, Hellie?' he says.

Mum says nothing.

'I'll go and get the boys,' I say.

I go into the sitting room where I can already hear the familiar sound of *The Wizard of Oz* coming from the TV. Maybe Finn will talk some sense into Harris and make him see that he should go for a different role in the school play . . .

But no. I enter the room to see that Harris has fast-forwarded to the scene where Dorothy, the Tin Man, the Lion and the Scarecrow are walking along the Yellow Brick Road. Finn has linked arms with Harris and they are prancing round and round the rug in front of the TV, singing, 'We're off to see the Wizaaard!' at the top of their voices. Pongo is following, wagging his tail as though he's about to take off.

How is a normal person supposed to live with this level of insanity?

I am about to raise my voice above the noise to let the boys know that we need to start our 'family meeting', when there is a howl from the kitchen.

Even the boys react to this. They stop singing, unlink their arms and speed past me.

'What's up?' Harris yells as he pushes me out of his way.

As I race the boys to the kitchen, I hear a strange rumble followed by a crack and then a rushing noise. I skid to a halt behind the boys as Finn cries, 'NO!'

Mum is crying, 'Can't you stop it, Rob?'

'I don't know! Where is it coming from?' he shouts.

Part of the ceiling has come away and water is gushing through the light fittings.

I know exactly where it is coming from – my bedroom!

I scamper up the stairs with Rob following close behind. We reach my bedroom door together to see that my whole room is flooded. Water is coming through the wall, over my bed and on to the carpet.

'What the—?' I gasp.

Rob puts his hands on my shoulders. 'Out the way,' he says, moving me to one side. 'Sorry!' he adds as he sprints back down the stairs and out of the front door, yelling, 'YUKIIIII!'

I stand, staring at my room. The carpet is soaked. Water is still coming through the wall – or to be more precise, through my BOOKCASE.

All my books are ruined.

Chapter Thirteen

Mum has ordered Finn and Harris to mop up the water in the kitchen while she and I have pulled all my books off the shelves. We are laying them out in the airing cupboard to try and salvage them. I am sobbing. Mum is tearful too.

'I am so sorry, Skye, darling,' she is saying, over and over.

I can't speak, I am crying so much. It is not Mum's fault anyway. The water was definitely coming from next door. Rob must have turned it off, though, because it's not pouring through the hole in the wall any more.

But my books! Will they survive this? Mum is trying to reassure me through her tears.

'Not all of them are wet, love. Only the ones on the bottom shelf. And they will dry out, I promise,' she says. 'I have dropped books in the bath before – the pages will be wrinkled, but they will be OK. Stop crying, sweetie. It will be all right.'

How did this happen? Rob has been doing a lot of work on their house, maybe he made a mistake with the plumbing. I knew he shouldn't have done all that work, changing Mrs Robertson's house around.

Then something else occurs to me: will this mean we can't move out until everything is fixed? Is that why Mum is crying too? Or does she really care that much about my books? I am sobbing too hard to say any of this out loud.

Eventually the wet books are fanned out in the warmth of the airing cupboard. I am still snuffling and shuddering from my crying fit, but Mum says we must go back downstairs.

'You can't stay in your room, anyway,' she says. 'I think you'll have to sleep in Harris's room tonight.'

'You are joking!' I cry. On top of this disaster she expects me to share a room with my little brother? 'Can't I at least sleep in your room?' I plead.

Mum shakes her head and tells me to dry my eyes as we go into the kitchen.

'Boys, well done!' Mum says, using her cheeriest voice. 'You've done a great job.'

'Mum, I am *not* sleeping in Harris's room tonight,' I say.

'We had to use every towel in the house. Sorry, Hellie,' says Finn.

'The mop doesn't work,' says Harris.

'Mum. Mum!' I try again. 'I'm NOT. Are you listening?'

Mum sighs as she takes in the pile of soggy, stained towels they have plonked in the sink. 'At least the water has stopped,' she says.

'MUM!'

Mum puts a hand on my shoulder. 'Skye, please. I know you're upset about your books, but there are more important things to worry about right now.'

'Yeah, like I think it might have to be brownies only for tea,' says Finn. He points at the lasagne ingredients, which are covered in flakes of ceiling paint and water. 'I'll chuck those, shall I?'

Mum nods.

'I don't mind having brownies instead of lasagne!' says Harris.

'You might when you taste them,' says Finn.

'Who CARES about what we are having for tea?' I shout. 'My bedroom is ruined and my BOOKS are ruined and I don't want to share a bedroom with my stupid little brother!'

Just as I yell this, Rob walks in with a sheepish Yuki in tow.

'Hey, guys,' she says. 'I was running a bath while I was in the shower. I guess I lost track of time.'

Everyone stares at her.

'You – you did this?' Mum says at last, gesturing at the mess.

Yuki holds up her hands. 'Hey, let's just chill a minute—'

Rob cuts her dead with, 'Yuki, just explain and apologize to Hellie.'

'It's not just me that's upset. It's Skye, too,' says Mum. 'Her room is flooded and some of her books are ruined.'

'Oh, honey!' Yuki says, her head on one side. 'Come here.' She opens her arms towards me.

Mum puts her arms around me and pulls me back so that Yuki can't hug me. I think that's a bit harsh. Yuki is only trying to be nice.

'I'm soooo sorry,' Yuki says. She puts her hands together as though in prayer, pleading with us to forgive her. 'I know your books mean everything to you, babe. What can I say? It was an accident. I was running a bath while I washed my hair in the shower. I was meditating and I must have lost track of time—'

'Why would you run a bath while you were in the shower?' Harris asks.

'It's one of Mum's crazy things she does,' Finn says.

Yuki looks Harris up and down. She is clearly thinking there are crazier people than her in the room right now, and she would be right. She doesn't comment on Harris's outfit though, which is amazing. But then I suppose she is very open-minded. She looks back at Finn.

'Angel, you know that baths are not something we do in eastern cultures. It is regarded as unacceptable to sit, lingering in dirty water,' says Yuki.

Mum looks at Rob with an incredulous expression.

'It's true,' Rob says, helplessly. 'The theory is that sitting in bath water when you are dirty is unhygienic, so you shower off the dirt first.'

I have never thought about it in that way, but actually that is a good idea. I increasingly feel as though Yuki is a breath of fresh air after the madness of my own family. I am furious about my books, but I can see it was an accident.

Mum looks up to the ceiling. 'Presumably you don't actually have to run a bath WHILE you are in the shower?' she says. 'Otherwise this would happen to everyone all the time.'

Yuki looks up too. 'Oh, man!' she says. 'I really have done it, haven't I?'

'I *did* ask you not to use that bathroom,' says Rob. 'The tiles were badly cracked. They needed ripping off and replacing. I was worried water had already got in behind them. I said all this, remember?' He glares at Yuki. 'Anyway, I thought you said you were just going to have a quick shower before coming over for supper?'

'I felt I needed to cleanse properly before we came together this evening,' Yuki says. 'You said this was going to be a big evening – it sounded like you were going to announce the start of a new chapter. A clean page for everyone.'

Rob glances at me, his forehead crinkling. 'Not a great choice of words, in the circumstances,' he says in a quiet voice.

'It's OK,' I mutter.

'We should get some food,' Mum says quickly changing the subject. 'It will have to be takeaway. I think the lasagne might be off the menu, now.'

'YAY! PIZZA!' says Harris. He pirouettes in Mum's red shoes and finishes off with a curtsey.

'I think the sparkling wine might be off the menu as well,' I mutter.

'Why's that? Looks fine to me,' Finn says, picking up the bottle.

Rob takes it from him. 'Excuse me, young man.'

'I'm not exactly in the mood for a celebration right now,' I say.

'Ye-es,' says Mum. 'Skye's right.'

'What are you *saying*?' Yuki coos. She goes over

to Mum and touches her on the arm. 'You have *so* much to celebrate, Hellie: lovely kids, a job, a great new relationship. And –' she gives Mum a knowing nudge – 'Rob tells me you and he are thinking of selling up and moving into a new place together. That is sooooo wonderful. Although . . .' she pauses and looks up at the ceiling again, her expression pained, 'I guess this little accident might have set that back a bit?'

Mum's face drains. 'Rob?' she says, glancing at him.

Rob looks as though he is struggling not to shout at someone. His expression is like clouds gathering before a storm.

Yuki seems to sense the tension and hastily carries on talking. 'Listen, babe. I know this accident has made a bit of a mess, but you can help with that, can't you, Rob? He's in the building trade after all,' she says to Mum.

'I know,' says Mum quietly.

'He knows his stuff,' Yuki goes on. 'And if we need to muck in a bit together while the work's being done, that's OK, isn't it?'

Mum says nothing.

'It will be OK, you'll see. It's only a bit of plaster and paint – material things. They are not important,' Yuki says, waving a hand dismissively. 'What *is* important is relationships. My guru talks about the interconnectedness of all living things—'

'Mum!'

'Yuki . . .'

Finn and Rob are both trying to stop Yuki, but she is clearly on a mission to cheer us all up. She continues:

'It won't do us any harm to squash in together for a while. People need to learn to live alongside one another more. It would be better for our souls – better for the planet – if we all shared more with the people we love. It's like I was saying the other day: my guru said this is why I haven't been able to create.'

Mum turns abruptly and catches the pile of estate agents' details that were on the edge of the table. They cascade on to the still-damp floor.

'Here, let me,' says Yuki, bending to pick them up. 'Life is a chain,' she says, as she collects up the soggy brochures. 'All things are related. When any link is harmed, the other links are affected.' She sighs and puts the brochures back on the table, smiling sadly at Rob.

Mum is still not saying anything. She has her back to us now and is gripping the side of the kitchen sink.

'What are you going on about, Yuki?' Rob says.

'*Family*, honey,' she replies. 'The interconnectedness of *family*. I broke the chain. I affected our links. That is why I cannot connect to my art any more. And that is why I have come back. To repair the chain.' She pauses, holding Rob's gaze.

'Rob,' Mum says, without turning round, 'are you going to sort this out?'

Finn, Harris and I are standing as still as statues. It is like we are watching a play unfold before us – one of those 'grown-up' plays that are impossible to understand because no one seems to be saying what they really mean.

'Okaaay,' says Rob. His voice is tight with the effort of keeping calm. 'Yuki. Can we – as you would say – just *rewind* a bit? The last time you came, you explained to us that "family was a tie" and that you couldn't be creative "within the walls of a marriage", I seem to remember.' He has a wild look in his eye that makes me think of an animal at the zoo, pacing its cage in a bid to escape. 'Things have moved on since then. Hellie and I—'

Yuki grabs the back of a chair. 'Yes!' she says, leaning forward. 'Things *have* moved on. That's just it! Life is about change, about flow and energy.' She lets go of the chair and starts moving her arms around to emphasize her point. 'We can't stand still, Rob, or we stagnate, like smelly water! We have to let ourselves be carried along the river of life. Look at Harris, here. He knows how to go with the flow. If a boy can wear a dress and not care how strange people think he is—'

Harris's expression darkens. 'I'm not strange,' he says.

'Yuki. Don't change the subject. You knew Hellie

and I wanted to start looking for a new house,' Rob says. 'This was what tonight was all about. We were going to show the kids some places we had seen.'

'Yeah, Yuki,' says Harris. He juts his chin out and puts his hands on his hips. 'We are going to move in together. We are going to be a proper family! I can't wait.'

Everyone is silent, waiting to see who will say what next. I can't speak at all. I can't even think properly. Is Yuki going to go ballistic? Is Mum? I need to leave. But I can't even go to my room, the state it's in. This evening is turning into a disaster movie: I am outside everything, watching a car crash in slow motion.

Rob puts his arm around Mum and says, 'Harris is right.'

Yuki gives a tight smile. 'Really?'

Mum's eyes are filling up and her cheeks are pink. 'Well, we're not going to be moving now, are we?' she says, her voice rising. 'No one is going to want to buy our houses with a massive hole in the wall and water damage everywhere.'

Rob looks awkward. 'Yes. I – I have to say it looks a lot worse over at our place. I guess we will all have to squash in here for a bit while I look into getting things fixed. Sorry, Hellie.'

'Oh, *man!*' Finn says. 'There's not enough room for

us in either house. We all have too much stuff and there is no way I am sharing a room.'

'Awww, but I want to share a room with you, Finn—' Harris begins.

'You can forget about *me* sharing!' I say.

Finn sneers. 'Don't worry, I wouldn't dream of it.'

Yuki bursts out laughing, making me jump. 'But, angel, don't you see? The bath overflowing, the hole in the wall – this is totally cosmic karma!'

'You're not making sense, Yuki, and you're not helping either.' Rob looks really angry now. 'In fact I think you should leave. Hellie is already really upset, the evening's been ruined. There is nothing "cosmically karmic" – or whatever – about any of this.'

'But Rob, honey. You are missing the point.' Yuki grabs Rob's arm. 'This is what I mean about going with the flow of life: you and Hellie want to be together, you want your families to be together – and now you don't need to wait around for a new house. You can just move in together straight away! Tonight! There's no time like the present. And don't worry about me. I can camp on the sofa. Oh my!' Her voice has gone up so many octaves she is squeaking. 'Talk about interconnectedness. This is just about as interconnected as it gets. All of us, in one place, in this house, all together. It was meant to be!'

Yuki springs away from Rob and launches herself at

Mum, who has taken a shaky step back and is pinned against the sink now. Yuki gets hold of Mum in an awkward embrace. Then she steps away from Mum and throws her arms wide at me, Finn and Harris. 'Come on, kids! You too.'

Harris shakes his head, his face thunderous.

'No,' says Rob. 'No hugs. And no more talking. Please, Yuki, we are all tired and upset. We need to finish clearing up and go to bed.'

'OK, I'll just go grab my things,' says Yuki.

'No,' says Rob. 'You stay at mine. You can have my room. It's the only bedroom that hasn't suffered any damage. The rest of us will stay here.' He makes a move towards Yuki forcing her back into the doorway.

'OK, OK, I'm going!' Yuki says. She bows deeply. 'Peace,' she says. Then turns and leaves us.

Mum lets her breath out as though she has been holding it in for a long time. Rob stretches out an arm towards her and pulls her into him.

'So guys,' Rob says, looking at me, Finn and Harris. 'I think Yuki is right about one thing: there is no time like the present. If we are serious about being a family, we might as well start tonight. What do you reckon? Are you ready?'

'YES!' says Harris, punching the air.

'I guess,' says Finn.

'Great!' says Rob. Then he kisses the top of Mum's head. 'Don't worry about the flood. We'll fix it, and then we can still sell the houses and move. Everything will be fine.'

Mum smiles and rests her head on Rob's shoulder. 'Thanks, darling,' she says.

I look at everyone. They are all smiling. Even Finn.

As for me, I don't think I will ever smile again.

Chapter Fourteen

I don't know how I managed to get any sleep last night. Everyone was excited about us moving in together except me. I couldn't even work out how I felt. I sat and ate my pizza in silence while Mum and Rob chattered excitedly about the houses they had viewed online and Finn and Harris asked questions. Because all the brochures were soaked, Mum fetched her laptop, and once we had finished eating, she and Rob found the houses they had bookmarked and we had to sit around and look at the pictures together. Harris and Finn came up with crazy things they said our new house should have.

'Let's have a swimming pool!' Harris said at one point.

'Yeah, on the roof!' said Finn.

Rob didn't try to calm them down, and Mum didn't say even say, 'Boys!' in that way she does when they are getting out of hand. I think they should have stepped in and told them to be more realistic in their expectations, if you ask me. At this rate I am not going to be the only disappointed one when we all have to move to another town to be able to afford anything half as nice as where we live now. All the big houses around here cost far too much – you don't have to be a genius to see that. Rob and Mum had been looking at places miles away from here – they just weren't making a point of saying that to us. But I was paying attention to the details on screen, rather than making stupid comments about swimming pools on roofs.

Rob did at last notice I was being quiet, and he tried to get me involved by saying, 'What about you, Skye? What would your dream house have? Maybe you should have a special room to keep all your books in – like your own personal library?'

'Like my *bedroom*, you mean? Before it was

ruined with bath water from your place,' I pointed out.

Rob blushed and didn't say anything more to me after that. Mum frowned at me, but she let it go.

I know that was a nasty thing for me to have said. I don't really know why I said it. It was pretty clear that Rob was angry with Yuki, and that Mum was trying hard to turn the evening around and make the best of things with us all squashed in together. But I am the one who is suffering the most. I have lost my personal space, and it looks as though the only way I am going to get it back is by moving far away to another town, leaving Aubrey and school and everything I love behind.

I am in my room writing this. There is nowhere else I can write in private. I certainly wasn't going to write my journal in Harris's room last night. I would literally die if my brother ever found this and read it.

I am trying not to look at the mess my room is in, and it is making me more and more upset, thinking of leaving it forever.

I don't want a special library. I want my bedroom with my favourite windowsill – where I am perched now, writing this.

I am not supposed to be in here. Rob says I should stay out of my room until he has time to 'assess the damage'. But he and Mum went next door after breakfast today to talk to Yuki and 'assess the damage' over there, so no one knows I am in here. No one except Harris and Finn. Anyway, Harris is watching *The Wizard of Oz* AGAIN and making Finn test him on the scene where Dorothy meets the Scarecrow – so they don't care what I'm doing.

They never care. Last night when I was sleeping (or trying to sleep) on a camp bed in Harris's room, I told him I didn't want to move house, and all he said was, 'You're boring, Skye. You never want anything to change, ever. I like Rob and I like Finn, and I think it would be cool to have a massive house somewhere new with all of us in it together. Dorothy went to a new place and she had loads of adventures. You never know what you are going to find if you are not brave enough to try new things.'

I told him to shut up and that he sounded like Mum.

I lay there then, staring at the ceiling, thinking I knew how Dorothy felt when she ran away: no one here understands me. Maybe it would be cool if a twister came and picked our house up and took us millions of miles away to another land: far away from Finn and Rob and all my problems. We could start again as the little family we always were. Just me, Harris and Mum – and all my books. But I would have to find a way of getting Aubrey to come too. I can't survive without her.

My phone vibrates as I am writing in my journal. It is Aubrey, FaceTiming. It is as though she has read my mind. She does this a lot. This is why I cannot live without her.

I will ask if I can go round to hers to escape this madhouse. I press the green button and wait for us to connect.

'Hey,' I say flatly, when her face appears.

'Hey!' Aubrey waves like a loony. 'You haven't

texted for hours, so I thought I should check that you are still alive.'

'Only just,' I say.

'Wow,' says Aubrey. 'You look seriously fed up. What's up?'

'Yuki flooded our house last night. And now we are really going to have to get on and move because it is insanely crowded here and I am sleeping on a camp bed in Harris's room.'

'WHAT?'

I go on to explain.

Aubrey's eyes and mouth grow wider and wider. 'All this happened last night and you didn't text me?' she says. 'I would have come round!'

'Thanks, but it was really hectic.' And Mum didn't want me to invite you, I think. But of course, I don't say it.

'By the way, when am I going to meet Yuki?' says Aubrey. 'I *wish* I had an artist for a mum instead of my lunatic parents who have – get this for über-freakoid behaviour – *set up the town's first ever Tolkien Appreciation Society*! It's going to be in the local paper and everything.' She waves her hands in the air and screams. 'Aaaargh! If you ask me the jet lag hasn't worn off yet. She and Dad are seriously bonkers at the moment.'

'Oh?' I doubt even Aubrey's family can take the

Seriously Bonkers Parent of the Year Award away from Mum right now.

'You won't *believe* what Mum and Dad have planned for this weekend,' Aubrey goes on. 'Dad has made a slideshow of all the photos from our tour of Middle-earth and Mum has invited the local Ring Nutters – apparently there are loads of them, Dad says – around here to watch it tonight. We have to dress up, obvs – HIDEOUS OUTFIT ALERT! – and she's got me and Cora making hobbit-themed snacks all afternoon. Save me!'

'That does sound like full-on mentalism,' I say. I am smiling in spite of my bad mood. 'Although a tiny part of me would rather be you than me right now. Fancy a swap?'

'Totally!' says Aubrey. 'Although I would rather just come round and hang out with you.' She pauses and looks coy, and then says. 'You'll never guess what – Zane FaceTimed me really early this morning!'

At that moment, a tall floaty figure appears behind Aubrey. A face looms close to the screen, pointy elf-ears clearly in view.

'Hello, Skye,' says Mrs Stevens, Aubrey's mum. 'Don't keep Aubrey too long, will you? We need to make some alterations to her costume, and she still has fifty honey-cakes and fifty *lembas* to make.'

Aubrey keeps a rather crazy grin fixed to her face until her mum leaves the room, then she collapses and groans.

'*See* what I have to put up with?' she says.

'The honey-cakes sound good,' I say. I am keen not to get her going on the subject of Zane again. 'Not sure about the *lembas* – remind me what they are again?'

Aubrey grimaces. 'It's kind of gross thin bread, which you have to wrap in leaves.'

'Oh yes – doesn't it save the hobbits' lives at some point?'

Aubrey's grimace widens. 'Well I would rather *die* than have to go through with this party for losers tonight,' she wails. 'Anyway, as I was saying. Zane and I talked for hours – it was way before anyone else was up in this loony asylum – and he promised he would ask his parents if they could come on holiday to the UK at Christmas . . .'

I stop listening. Oh my life. Aubrey is such a nightmare when she has a crush. This boy is never going to come all the way from America to have a full-on romance with her. I can't handle this.

'Isn't that just epic?' she finishes.

'Yeah,' I say. 'Whereas *this* –' I show her the hole in the wall behind me – 'is the total opposite of epic. I can't bear it, Aubrey! I can't spend another night in Harris's room. He snores and his feet smell so bad I had to breathe through my mouth all night.' It is my turn to do some wailing now, and I need my best friend to stop wibbling about a boy on the other side of the ocean and give me some sympathy.

'In that case, moving to another house is a great idea!' says Aubrey. 'Your new bedroom will probably be twice the size – EVERYTHING will be twice the size because your new family is twice the size it was,' she says.

I know she is only trying to make me feel better, but she is totally missing the point.

'Yeah, but firstly my room wouldn't be the *same*. I bet I never get a room with a lovely window seat like this one. In any case, no one has definitely said I will even *have* my own room in our new place. Mum might say, "The bedrooms are so big, you can share with Harris permanently." And let me tell you *I would die* if I had to do that. Or – oh no!' A blood-chilling thought had just struck me.

'What?' says Aubrey.

'What if they make me share with Finn?'

'Oh wow. I would totally do that. Could I move in?'

'Aubrey!'

'Only joking. I'm not into him any more. Not now I have Zane. He is soooo lush—'

'AND SECONDLY,' I butt in, 'we are never going to be able to afford a big enough house around here.

Which means we'll have to move miles away, probably.'

I pause to see if that piece of news has any effect on my best friend: like making her maybe realize that she might actually miss me? What happened to all that 'you can't move' stuff she said when I first told he about this NIGHTMARE?

Just to prove how little she gets my problems, her eyes light up and she says, 'Hey! I've just had the most awesome thought – imagine the parties you could have in a big house? And you might even be allowed more pets. You've always said you would like rabbits and guinea pigs. The garden would be twice the size.'

'Aubrey,' I say sharply. 'I have not wanted rabbits or guinea pigs since I was eight.'

She looks over her shoulder suddenly, and I see a figure appear behind her.

'It's Cora,' she says. 'I've gotta go. Honey-cake duty awaits.' She pulls another face. 'Listen, it'll all work out, Skye. You worry too much. See you at school!'

And the screen goes dead.

'*You worry too much.*' Easy for her to say. She only has to get through one night of mortification with her family. I am going to have a lifetime of it if Mum and Rob get their way. And, the way things are looking, it's going to be without the love and support of my best friend.

Chapter Fifteen

The rest of the weekend has been awful. Aubrey has been busy the whole time with the Tolkien Appreciation Society, and I have spent hours moving all my things into Harris's room because the flood is making my room smell musty and gross. I was really grumpy about having to squash in with my little brother, especially when he made a huge effort to welcome me (NOT) by doing idiotic immature things such as farting and leaving a hairbrush inside my makeshift bed. Finn thought this was the most hilarious thing anyone had ever done to another human being and gave Harris a long list of other things he should try doing, like setting booby traps for me every time I come in his room. I told him that if we were all going to live together he was going to have to

make an effort to be less of an idiot. He told me
I would have to make an effort to be less of
a 'moody mare'. I wish Aubrey and the girls at
school could see what a totally immature waste
of space Finn is at home. They wouldn't all fall
at his feet, giggling and flicking their hair around
if they could see the real him in action.

And then there has been the singing and the
dancing. ALL WEEKEND.

If I hear 'Somewhere Over the Rainbow' just
one more time, that is exactly where I will be
drop-kicking my brother.

Yuki came round at one point to ask what the
noise was. She said that, on balance, she thought
she preferred Finn's drumming to the sound of
Harris singing. Mum got cross and told her that
Harris needed to practise.

'What is Harris wearing?' Yuki asked at one
point.

Mum bristled. 'Harris is very keen on getting
the part of Dorothy in the school play, so he is
staying in character all weekend. I think it's an
excellent idea. A lot of the best actors do that,
you know,' she added.

Yuki smiled and said, 'Yes, a lot of the *best* ones do. But most of them aren't nine-year-old boys. In any case, wouldn't you be better off going for a part you are more likely to get, baby?' she said to Harris. 'You'd make an excellent Scarecrow.' She giggled when she said that.

To be fair, Harris does look more like the Scarecrow than Dorothy right now. He has not changed out of the blue-and-white-checked apron outfit in two days, and the whole thing is looking pretty crumpled, especially the bow in his hair. He has not even changed out of it at night. I tried telling him I would have nightmares about being attacked by the Wicked Witch of the West, but he just put on a squeaky Dorothy voice and said, 'Don't worry about her. Glinda has given me a potion. I'll protect you!'

At least Mum put her foot down when Harris wanted Pongo to sleep in the room with us.

I am worried about Harris's audition. I think Mum should talk to him and try to manage his expectations. The way she is talking, it's like it's a done deal that he will get the part of Dorothy. Leaving aside his awful singing, I just can't see that happening. It was awful when he was bullied about the dancing last term. I just don't think Woodfield Primary is ready for a male Dorothy, however cute Harris looks in those sparkly shoes – something I am NEVER going to admit to him, by the way, especially if he doesn't stop making the word 'Some-where!' sound like Pongo howling when he's been shut outside.

I checked on my books this morning, and Mum was right – they have mostly dried out. They were all fatter than they had been, as though someone had inflated them with a bicycle pump – and their pages had yellowed and gone crinkly – but I could still read them. A few had quite damaged covers, which made me sad, but otherwise I think they will survive.

As I put them in boxes and carried them into Harris's room, I caught sight of *The Family from One End Street* by Eve Garnett. It is a very old-fashioned story about six children who have to share everything: bedrooms, clothes, toys. It was one of the books that Mrs Robertson gave me. I remember her telling me that her mother had come from a family like that, and that she had been overwhelmed when she had moved into this road, saying the house was a palace.

And there I was, moaning about sharing with Harris. *Maybe Aubrey is right and 'it will all be worth it in the end'*, I thought. *Maybe I am being spoilt . . .*

I changed my mind, however, when the most embarrassing thing *of my whole entire life* happened last night.

I got up to go to the bathroom and walked in on Rob who was SITTING ON THE LOO!

He was sitting in there in the dark, so we both screamed when I put on the light! Why on earth didn't he put the light on? I didn't really feel like stopping to ask him, though - SEEING AS HE WAS ON THE LOO! At least I would have known someone was in there if the light was on. I know he can't lock it. That is kind of my fault, as there has not been a lock on our bathroom door since I broke it when I shut myself in there last term - yet another mortifying incident in my life, which I have already written about in my journal, so I'm certainly not going to put myself through thinking about that again.

I am going to have to insist that Mum puts a lock on the door this week. I need to find a moment to talk to her about it in private though. I can't mention it in front of Rob. That would mean explaining that I had SEEN HIM ON THE LOO!

Writing it down is not making it any easier to cope with.

How Aubrey can think anything is worth having to live like this is beyond me. She doesn't get it at all. She has been sending me excited texts like this all morning:

> Can't stop thinking about HUGE HOUSES. It will be AMAZINGNESS! Parties! Massive bedroom! Ask if Rob can put a hot tub in the new garden – which will also be MAHOOOSIVE, obvs. 😊 🎈

I have been ignoring her while I write in my diary, but I am going to text back now, because I need her to get off my case about the whole party thing:

> Can u stop with all the MAHOOOSIVE HOUSE stuff? I DON'T WANT TO MOVE! WE MIGHT HAVE TO GO MILES AWAY! I CAN'T DO IT! 😿

She is taking ages to answer. I watch as the 'thought bubble' bobs around the screen, while Aubrey composes her text. Sometimes it would seriously be quicker for me to actually walk around to her house and speak to her face-to-face than wait for one of her über-long thoughtful-mode replies.

I am waiting.

And waiting.

There are still no actual words appearing on the screen.

Suddenly the phone rings, making me drop it and shriek in surprise. I see Aubrey's face and name staring up at me and scrabble to answer.

'What are you DOING?' I cry into the phone.

'It's me!' Aubrey says.

'I know *that*, you loony. I can see. And hear.'

'It's your best friend in the entire universe,' she says,

as though ignoring what I have just said. And I realize she is sounding strange, like she is trying not to cry or maybe get really angry.

'Ye-es,' I say. 'And you always will be. Are you OK?' I reach for the Maori pendant Aubrey gave me and hold on to it.

'NO!' she wails. 'And I will never be OK again if you MOVE MILES AWAY.'

'What? Why are you freaking out like this? I did tell you this the other day. I thought you understood – I have been trying to talk to you about how awful it's going to be, but you didn't seem that bothered,' I say.

'I know! I've only just realized! I have been such a dweeb, going on and on about my holiday and Zane – who by the way has only just texted me to say I am DUMPED.'

'Oh, that's bad—'

'Yes, it is very bad – especially since I had started saving up to go to America at Christmas.'

'Seriously?' Aubrey can be almost as insane as my mum sometimes. 'You will never have enough money to do that,' I say.

'I KNOW! But now I feel like I don't even care, because NOTHING can be as bad as you MOVING MILES AWAY!' she shrieks.

'Aubrey, calm down. We haven't even found a place

yet. And no one is going to want to buy our house or Rob's until the flood damage has been fixed. It is a nightmare, yes, but I'm not going anywhere yet. Stop crying!'

I am now going to have to spend ages calming Aubrey down and promising her something I am not in a position to promise at all, which is that I won't move miles away from her. Even as I am talking to her, I realize that she is probably much more upset about being dumped by The American, and that all her wailing and crying about losing me is not the main point of her call, but actually it is so nice to talk to her and tell her how I am feeling too, that I don't really care what her real reason was for phoning.

Eventually we say goodbye.

'See you at school,' Aubrey says, sniffing.

'Not if I see you first,' I say – which is one of those lame things we always say to each other.

I put my phone in my pocket and feel a weird mixture of sad and happy. It is annoying that it has taken this long for Aubrey to figure out what is going on with my life. She is just not on the same planet as me sometimes – so it is a relief to have her back again and actually listening to me.

My phone pings again. I get it out and see it is an afterthought text from Aubrey:

Am soz about blubbing. Also v soz about your books. 😞 You can always buy more tho! 📚 Wish I could buy a new boyfriend. JOKES! ☺ Hey – have just had epic idea! U could get a Kindle! 😊

I text back immediately:

AS IF!

She answers:

Yeah, yeah. I knew you'd hate that. 😕 See ya later ☺

Thank the heavens above for Aubrey Stevens. She is insane, and sometimes even a bit annoying, but she knows how to make me smile, even when I am feeling really low.

Aubrey's teasing about me getting a Kindle has got me thinking about books, and that has got me thinking about Mrs Robertson again and how much I miss her. Aubrey knows I am TOTALLY NOT a Kindle type of person. For me, nothing can replace a real book. Books don't need recharging.

Books have their own particular smell. Plus I like remembering who gave me which book and when . . .

Like Mrs Robertson, who gave me most of the books I own. Some of them are really old, so it wouldn't work for me to just buy more. I know I could ask for the same stories, but they wouldn't have the same old-fashioned covers, unless I was lucky enough to find them in a charity shop, and they wouldn't be the ones that Mrs Robertson had read to me when I was small.

Well, writing that down about Mrs Robertson has kind of helped me sort my mind out: it has made me decide once and for all that I am going to visit her as soon as I can. I will get the bus after school this week if Mum won't take me. I know I have promised Aubrey that I won't move miles away, but if Rob and Mum have their way, I might have to break that promise. I need some good advice, and Mrs Robertson is the only person I can think of right now who will listen to me properly.

Chapter Sixteen

I go straight to the library when I get to school. I can't face talking to anyone, not even Aubrey – especially as I suspect she is not done with talking about Zane yet. She texted me this morning with a load of angry emojis and comments about 'men' being an alien species. I can't handle any more of that right now. I need time to myself. In any case, I need to choose a book to read as I still can't read any of the ones I own.

There are a couple of newbie Year 7s in a corner on beanbags, reading – otherwise the place is very quiet. Mrs Ball doesn't seem to be around yet, so I decide to see if she's got any new books in. Sometimes she has a clear-out of the library over the summer and gives some old books to charity to make room for shiny new ones. I go to the 'New Books' section to have a browse.

I can't find *The Amber Spyglass*, which is what I really wanted to read next. I guess it must still be on order. I pick out *The Declaration* by Gemma Malley instead. I am soon engrossed. It is a scary futuristic story in which someone has discovered an elixir for long-lasting life, so everyone is living for years and years. This means that the government has said no one can have children, as there is not enough of everything to go around now that the population is ageing and not dying. Any children that exist have had to go underground. It's a bit like I imagine it must have been for people in hiding in the Second World War: some of the book makes me think of Anne Frank's diary, which describes living in hiding so well it gave me nightmares when I read it. *The Declaration* has got me hooked. I am completely in the world of the main character, Anna, and am oblivious to anything going on around me.

Which means that I am completely freaked when I hear a voice very close to me say:

'What are you reading?'

'Wha—?' I give a ridiculously loud gasp and leap up from the beanbag I am sitting on as though someone has poured cold water down my back.

'Sorry, Skye.'

It is Effi. He has crept up behind me (he must have done – I didn't hear a thing) and is leaning over my shoulder, looking at the book.

Except he is not any more, as I have smacked him in

the face with my book by leaping up so suddenly.

'Sorry,' he says again, rubbing his nose. 'I did not mean to frighten you.'

'No, I – I'm sorry,' I stammer. 'I didn't mean to hit you. Are – are you OK?'

He nods and his face relaxes into a broad grin, showing off those ultra-white teeth. 'Nothing broken – at least, I don't think so,' he says. He makes a big deal out of checking his fingers and arms and brushing himself down. 'Maybe one day you will say "hi" without trying to knock me out!' he jokes.

I blush and cannot think of a thing to say other than 'sorry' again.

Effi laughs. 'So what *are* you reading? It must be good. You were lost in another world.'

My heart gives a little leap. 'Yes. That's *exactly* where I was,' I say. No one at school ever asks me what I am reading – except Mrs Ball, of course. And no other kid my age has ever shared with me that feeling of being lost in a story before.

He nods towards my copy of *The Declaration*. 'I don't know it. What's it about?'

'Erm, it's kind of futuristic,' I say. 'And dark.'

Effi's eyes shine. 'Sounds like sci-fi. Is it? I love sci-fi!' he says. 'Tell me more.'

'Well, it's not exactly sci-fi. Mrs Ball calls it

"dystopian" fiction,' I say. 'There are no aliens or anything, but I guess there is science in it – kind of.' I start to babble about the plot. 'I think I like it coz the adults are the evil ones and the kids are the goodies. I like books where the adults either disappear altogether or they are useless or evil.'

Effi looks immediately very serious. 'Wow.' He doesn't seem to know what else to say.

I feel like an idiot for getting so heavy. 'I guess, what I mean is, books are more fun if the kids are in control.'

Effi nods. 'Yes. I understand that,' he says.

'What do you like to read?' I ask.

'My favourite book is *The Hitchhiker's Guide to the Galaxy*. Do you know it?' he asks.

'No,' I say. 'Never heard of it.'

Effi's eyes grow wide. 'You haven't? It is one of the best science-fiction books ever written.'

I twist my mouth. 'Hmmm, that'll be why I haven't read it, then,' I say. 'I am not really into sci-fi.'

Effi pulls up a beanbag and sits down next to me. 'But you like this book,' he says, pointing to *The Declaration*. 'That is in the future and has a scientific theme, no? In any case, *The Hitchhiker's Guide* is so much more than sci-fi,' he says.

A group of Year 11s walk in as he is talking. They turn to glare at us.

I put my finger to my lips. 'We'll have to whisper,' I tell Effi. 'We're not allowed to talk in here while people are studying.'

Effi glances at the Year 11s and shuffles closer to me, leaning in. A faintly spicy scent comes off him. It is like forests and night-time . . .

What? Why does my brain do freaky things when I talk to Effi? I tell myself to listen to what he is saying.

'It's one of those books that you can read over and over again,' he is saying. 'Do you do that?'

'I, erm . . .' It is quite off-putting, sitting so close to a boy I didn't know very well, whispering about books. Especially when he smells really nice.

ARGH! CONCENTRATE!

Effi's forehead crinkles. 'I suppose that is stupid of me to say,' he says. 'Why would you read something more than once? It is a waste of time, isn't it?'

'No, no. Of course, I do!' I say, a bit too loudly.

'Shhhh!' One of the Year 11s hisses at me, and the others giggle.

Effi ignores them. 'So which books do you go back to then?' he asks.

My turn to feel stupid. 'Well, they are kind of babyish . . . but the point is they are books that comfort me, so that's why I go back to them.' I pause.

'Tell me,' Effi says.

I clear my throat. '*The Lion, the Witch and the Wardrobe* for when I am feeling sad and lonely – or any of the Harry Potters, obviously – that goes without saying. Oh, and *Pippi Longstocking* for when I want a laugh.' I am warming to my theme. The thing is, it is practically impossible for me to choose a favourite book, and there are loads that I have read again and again, including a very old one of Mum's called *Felicia the Critic* by Ellen Conford, which I love. It is about a girl a bit younger than me who just doesn't get her sister, who is – guess what – thirteen. Felicia tries to solve people's problems by pointing out what they are doing wrong, but she is not at all subtle, so is always getting into trouble. It is a very funny book, but also moving, as you know that Felicia is only trying to help. She just doesn't understand why she makes people so cross. I don't suppose he will have heard of that one, though, so I wibble on about Pippi for a bit longer.

Effi is laughing, but in a good way – not *at* me, like people usually do. I can tell this because his eyes are sparkly and his face is kind.

He is talking about his favourite books now. 'Oh yes, I love Pippi – she is crazy! She has a horse in her house! And . . . wait, she makes pancakes on the floor, no? My favourite chapter is when she goes to school. She is very naughty and confuses and annoys the teacher.' He chuckles.

I must look surprised because Effi goes on to say, 'My father teaches English. We have always had a lot of English and European books in our house.'

'Cool! I love Pippi,' I say. 'She is just so confident and sure that she is the one with all the answers. Even when she has lost her dad and has to live alone.' I wish I could be like that.

Thinking about Pippi makes me think about my own dad, whom I can't remember, and then I find I am thinking about Mum and Rob and the whole move thing. I have managed not to think about it while we were talking. I shift on the beanbag.

Effi's voice breaks into my thoughts. 'It is hard to face change,' he says. He sounds sad.

I stiffen. It is as though he has read my mind. Only Aubrey can do that.

He is staring at the far wall. 'I didn't want to come to this place,' he says. 'I miss my friends. And it is so cold here.' He looks as though he is going to say something else, but he just smiles sadly and shakes his head.

'Go on,' I say.

He looks up at me. 'My dad was offered a wonderful job at the university. We could not turn it down. I am sure I will be fine.'

'Where is home?' I ask him, just for something to say.

Effi grins. 'Nigeria. The most beautiful place in the world.' Then his face falls and he says, 'But now home is here. Number sixty-four Waverley Road.'

'That's near me! You should come round some time.' What did I say that for? He is going to think I am a complete creep. I hardly know the guy.

But Effi's wide white-toothed grin is back. 'That would be so nice,' he says. 'Perhaps I could borrow your copy of *Pippi*? I had to leave most of my books at home – I mean, in Nigeria. I did bring *HG2G* with me, though. You can borrow it in return if you like?'

'Borrow what?' I ask, confused.

'*HG2G – The Hitchhiker's Guide to the Galaxy*,' Effi says. 'It is what fans call it.'

I feel a sudden rush of happiness. It seems to come from nowhere. I think it must be because Effi seems to completely understand how excited I am, talking about my favourite books. He seems to love this 'Hitchhiker' thing so much that he needs to share it – with someone who loves books too.

I suddenly realize that he has asked me a question. And that I am staring at him.

'Are you OK?' Effi asks.

'I – yeah. Sorry.'

'Ah good. So you will come to the gig on Friday?' he says.

'Gig? Friday?'

'Yes. I was saying – the Electric Warthogs have the first gig of the term. Although I think it will be more like a rehearsal really. We "totally suck",' he says, hooking his fingers around the words. 'This is what Finn says, which means we are not very good, I think. But the others are sure we should do it.' He chuckles. 'I thought Finn might have asked you to come and watch us.' He seems to look deeper into my eyes when he says this.

Heat rushes to my face. Why am I blushing now? Effi will think I have a thing for Finn. Imagine that gossip: Did you hear? Skye Green has a crush on her mum's boyfriend's son – eeuwww!

The more I tell myself not to blush, the redder I feel myself become.

Effi frowns slightly. 'Are you sure you are OK? Finn told me you had a bad weekend. He texted me . . .' he tails off and looks away.

'What did he say?' I snap without meaning to.

Now Effi looks as uncomfortable as I feel. 'I am sorry. It is none of my business,' he says. I think he is about to walk away, then he says, 'I suppose Finn is talking to me because I have told him that I know what it is like when things change in a family.' He pauses. 'You can talk about it to me, if you like? I would not say anything to Finn.'

The bell rings.

Effi shoves his hands into his pockets. 'OK. I had better go. Maybe I will see you later?' He smiles.

My stomach does a weird flip. 'Sure,' I say.

He nods and turns to go.

My mind is reeling with how nice he is being and thoughts of Finn talking to him about my mum and his dad and how many other people he has talked to about it and how Aubrey isn't taking me seriously, so maybe I should talk to Effi. But the more I think about that, the more I realize how lonely I feel. I can't talk to someone I hardly know. Especially a boy.

Especially one who makes me feel so strange when I sit too close to him.

Chapter Seventeen

I am writing this on the bus on the way to see Mrs Robertson. When Effi brought up the subject of Finn talking to him, I realized I needed to talk to someone too. But I can't talk to him. And Aubrey has gone into über-depressed mode over Zane. She told me she was thinking of wearing only black and staying in her room until she hears from him. Apparently he will not answer any of her texts or messages. I wonder why . . . NOT. Even I know that when a boy dumps you, that means they do not want ANY contact with you ever again. I hope she is not going to turn into some kind of international stalker. If I were Zane I would change my phone number. And possibly my name and address. But then, if I were Zane I would not have been idiotic enough to start a holiday romance with someone who lives on another continent and takes holiday romances as seriously as marriage proposals.

I texted Mum earlier and told her I was going to see Mrs R after school. I can't wait any longer. Mum keeps saying she will take me herself, but whenever I ask, all I get is, 'It's not a good time, Skye.' So? It is NEVER going to be a 'good time' at this rate. I had already looked up the bus timetable online ages ago, and the care home is only a few stops on from school. Mum said it was OK as long as I texted her every five minutes to let her know I was still alive. (Hashtag parental paranoia.)

I think Mum might be feeling a tiny bit guilty about me sharing with Harris, actually. I screamed at him this morning because he came in without knocking while I was getting dressed for school and then announced to everyone (including Rob, Finn and Yuki, of course) that I was wearing a pink bra and yellow pants. Even Mum told him off after that.

It's not my fault that I can't find matching stuff. Everything is a mess at our place right now.

I am surprised I can find any underwear at all. So I suppose things could be worse. (Not MUCH.)

The bus has arrived outside the care home. It is called Oakswood House. I am quite surprised at how modern it is: lots of glass – not dark and dingy and depressing, as I had imagined it would be. Right, time to get off . . .

It still doesn't look like anyone's actual home. When I am shown into Mrs Robertson's neat and tidy little room, it feels like I am visiting someone in a hotel, not sitting with an old friend in their comfy sitting room. It makes me feel sadder than ever.

Mrs Robertson is in a chair by the window, looking out at a bird feeder that is right outside. That is a nice thing for someone to have done, but I still can't help thinking how different all this is from her old house. When she lived next to us she had plants in the window boxes and flowery curtains, and she sat in an armchair by the fireplace so that you could see her white head bent over a book or some sewing if you looked in through the window.

All that has changed, of course. Rob has made the front room into an extension of the kitchen – or he had started to before the flood. I don't suppose he'll bother finishing that now that we are going to move.

Mrs Robertson is reading when I knock on the door. She looks up and gives a little start.

'Skye, dear! How lovely to see you. My goodness, you've—' She stops herself and puts a shaky hand to her mouth.

'Grown?' I say, smiling. When anyone else says that, it annoys me, but nothing Mrs Robertson says ever has.

She nods and lets her hand drop to her lap. 'I am sorry. I am sure everyone says "you've grown". It used to make me so fed up when people said it to me – as if you hadn't noticed it yourself! These days people are more likely to tell me, "My, how you've shrunk!"' She gives a dry chuckle. Her already lined face crinkles even more as she smiles, her black-bead eyes disappearing into the map of wrinkles. She looks so fragile; as if she is made of worn paper that would disintegrate at a touch. It reminds me of my poor, puffed-up, yellowing books.

I immediately feel bad. 'I am sorry that it has taken me so long to come and visit,' I say.

Mrs Robertson shakes her head and says, 'Nonsense!' very firmly. And in that moment, she looks less like a tiny old lady and more like my lovely friend again.

I relax.

She asks after Mum and Harris, and questions me about school.

'Got a boyfriend yet?' she teases. 'Oh! You're blushing – who is he?'

'I don't have a boyfriend,' I say. A picture of Effi, standing in the library, telling me about the Hitchhiker's book swims before my eyes, and I know I am blushing even more. I am such an idiot! I wouldn't even say he was a friend, let alone a boyfriend. I hardly know him. And I'm not getting on very well with *HG2G*, as he calls it. I borrowed it from the library, but I can't get into it. It's too weird for me.

Mrs Robertson is watching me carefully, but she simply smiles and nods and asks me what I am reading.

I tell her about *HG2G*, but she has never read it. Then I tell her that I much prefer *The Subtle Knife*, which is not a book she knows either, but she always loves to find out about books she hasn't heard of. Then I tell her that Mrs Ball has been encouraging me to write.

'Ah, you are very lucky to have such a good school librarian,' says Mrs Robertson. 'It was a librarian who encouraged me with my reading – but I've told you about that.'

She has, but I tell her I don't mind her repeating old stories.

'There's my Skye,' Mrs Robertson says. 'Always loved stories of any shape or size, didn't you? But why don't you tell me about the story *you* are writing?'

'It's not really a story,' I tell her. 'More a journal of my ideas and feelings.' Then I sigh. If only life were as easy as a story, I think.

She peers at me closely. 'You don't seem very happy, dear. Is there something on your mind?'

Then, with an almost physical sense of relieving myself of a huge burden, I plunge in and tell her everything that has happened since she moved out: how Mum and Rob fell in love and how they kept it secret for ages; how I don't like having Finn around all the time; how things are not really the same between Aubrey and me any more; and how Yuki is back, which seems to make everyone irritable – everyone except me, that is. Finally I tell her about Rob and Mum's plans to move house.

Mrs Robertson sits and listens patiently. I am not sure I am being a very entertaining or cheery visitor. Mrs Robertson always used to tell me how important it was to 'smile and the world smiles with you'. She had a favourite quote from Roald Dahl's *The Twits*, which she would use when I was feeling down: 'If a person has ugly thoughts, it begins to show on the face.' The thought of ending up looking like one of the Twits was usually enough to get me to smile. It doesn't seem to work these days, though. I guess I have bigger worries than I did when I was small.

Mrs Robertson lets me finish, then she takes my hand

and squeezes it. 'You know, once upon a time . . .' she begins.

'Once upon a time', here we go, I think. She is going to tell me a story to make me feel better.

'. . . I was a bit like your mum.'

Wow! I wasn't expecting that.

I must look dubious because Mrs Robertson laughs a crackly, wheezy laugh and says, 'I never told you about my first husband, did I?'

Talk about a good opening line!

'*First* husband?' I repeat. 'Why, how many have you had?' immediately thinking how rude that sounds.

Luckily Mrs Robertson laughs again and assures me she has had 'only two'. Then she asks me to go to the chest of drawers and get out a 'tatty green' photo album.

I find the right one – dark green, frayed at the edges and so ruffled and used that I worry it might fall apart. I bring it over to Mrs Robertson and she talks me through the photos inside. They are taken in black and white and are mostly of a wedding. I can tell right away that the bride is Mrs Robertson: she has the same smile. She and the groom are looking into each other's eyes in such an intense way that you would think everyone around them has vanished and that they are the only two people left on the planet.

'You look beautiful,' I tell her.

Mrs Robertson chuckles and says, 'People did tell me I was a bit of a stunner in those days.'

She closes her eyes and falls silent.

I feel awkward. Has she fallen asleep? Old people do that quite suddenly sometimes, I know. I wonder if I should creep out and leave her in peace . . .

Then suddenly her eyes pop open again and she says, 'Bill died in an accident at work. He fell from some scaffolding. He lay in a coma for a long time. But in the end, there was nothing they could do.' Her voice becomes quieter as she goes on to tell me, 'I was only nineteen and I was expecting Fred, my oldest son.' She finds a later photo and points a shaky finger at a faded picture of a blond toddler on a tricycle outside a house. 'That's Fred,' she says.

He is so cute. He has light hair, appley cheeks and chubby arms, and a wonderful smile, very much like Mrs Robertson's. I am about to say so, when I recognize the house.

'Hey! That's our house!' I say. 'I mean – your old house and my house. I can see the window boxes you always had, and that's the apple tree, isn't it?' I look more closely at the photo and notice something strange. 'But – there's only one door.'

I look up at Mrs Robertson. She is beaming again and nodding. She congratulates me on having such sharp eyes. 'Yes, Bill and I bought the whole thing for a song all those years ago,' she tells me.

I am confused. 'I don't get it. You mean both the houses were yours? *Both* halves? But how come you only ever lived in one part of it? I mean, we are in the other half.' I am getting in a total muddle now.

Mrs Robertson winks. 'That was then,' she says cryptically, and then she sits back, looking wistful. 'Bill and I had planned to have lots of children,' she says. 'We were going to fill all the bedrooms with the patter of tiny feet. But when I was left a widow with just one child, I couldn't afford to keep the house going. So after a while I found a builder and paid him to divide it in two. It was easier to do that kind of thing back then. Not so many rules and regulations as there are now.'

As she tells me more about the building work, I am only half listening. All I can think is: our house has only ever been *half* a house. I don't really know why, but it makes me think about what Yuki said when she talked about 'karma'. I always wondered why I had felt so at home in Mrs Robertson's half. Now it seems I know why: it *was* part of my home.

'Fred never liked the fact that I changed things,' Mrs Robertson is saying. 'He was only five, but he never really forgave me for "cutting our house in half". He was a boy who struggled with change, poor little man. When I met

Albert when Fred was ten, that was the last straw for my poor Fred.' She looks so sad when she says that. 'Albert was a lovely stepdad to Fred, of course, but Fred never got over me having Roger and Lily, my other children.'

I don't know what to say to that. 'I – I'm sorry,' I mutter.

'Don't you worry, my dear,' she says, patting my hand. 'It is all water under the bridge. Things changed when Fred became a father himself. He told me he understood me better, and we get along fine now. Families are tricky things, Skye,' she says. 'They come in all shapes and sizes. Like houses,' she says.

'It's weird imagining you moving into that huge house all those years ago,' I say.

'You mean you can't imagine me being young?' Mrs Robertson teases.

'N-no,' I protest. Then I stop. I don't really know what I am imagining. I am trying to get my head around everything she has told me about her life: all that stuff I didn't know. Why hasn't she told me before about her and Bill and Fred and the fact both our houses once belonged to her?

She holds up the book she was reading when I arrived.

'You remember this one, don't you?' she asks, breaking the silence.

It is *The Little Prince* by Antoine de Saint-Exupéry.

'Of course! I love it.' I wonder why she is changing the subject.

'Do you remember that lovely quote?' she says.

'The story is full of great quotes!' I say. 'You might have to give me a clue which one you're thinking of.'

'"All grown-ups were once children . . . but only a few of them remember it."' She pauses and smiles. 'Maybe you need to be less hard on your mum and the choices she makes, Skye. She was your age once. And you might not believe it, but perhaps she doesn't feel much of a grown-up deep down inside. It is quite possible that she is finding all the changes just as hard to adjust to as you are.'

I pull a face. I doubt it.

Mrs Robinson gives me a knowing look and touches my arm. 'And another thing,' she says. 'Seeing as I'm in the mood to give advice: some endings are actually beginnings in disguise.'

'Is that from *The Little Prince* too?' I ask.

'No,' she says. 'That one is from here.' She taps her head and winks at me, then sighs and closes her eyes again.

This time she does fall asleep, very quickly. I am worried that I have worn her out, so I decide to leave her in peace. But before I creep out of the room, I tear a page from my diary and write her a quick note.

Thank you for listening to me, Mrs Robertson. I promise I will talk to Mum - and listen to her side of things, too. Maybe this IS going to be a new beginning. I will let you know!
Lots of love,
Skye
xxx

Chapter Eighteen

I am on the bus, on the way home. I really, really want to talk to Aubrey now, but when I texted her, saying I had something important to discuss, all she texted back was:

> Can't talk now. Zane about to Skype!!!! 😊 ♥

So much for being hysterical about the possibility of me moving. And so much for being dumped. Looks like I am on my own again, therefore I have decided to tell Mum about all the things I have just discovered. Mrs Robertson has made me see things differently. I don't want to end up like Fred and falling out with my mum. Mrs Robertson is right. I need to see things from Mum's point of view and I need to talk to her more. I am going to try to get her alone so that we can have a proper heart-to-heart. I am also going to listen to what she has to say. I feel bad about this, but I must admit that it had not occurred to me that Mum might be upset about change or find it difficult like me. I just thought she was so über-loved up with Rob that she didn't care about anything else. Bit like someone else I know.

So, I have decided I will let Mum talk to me about her feelings, and I will not get moody or interrupt or run upstairs or slam any doors. I will be grown-up and mature.

I push open the front door, grinning. I am buzzing with my newly formed good intentions and running through in my head how my cosy chat with Mum is going to pan out.

However, the second I step over the threshold my brain is immediately invaded by a barrage of noise coming from the kitchen.

This is the trouble with planning how conversations are going to go: it is fine when you are the only one in charge, working it all through in your head. Reality is almost always different. For example, I had not banked on there being a houseful of people when I got in. Goodness knows why I had not thought of this. This house is ALWAYS full of people these days.

There are certainly lots of voices talking over each other – and to make matters worse, none of them sounds particularly happy. The buzzing in my chest settles to a low, depressed hum, and my smile vanishes. I don't know what I was thinking, planning a nice quiet heart-to-heart with Mum. When was the last time I had an opportunity for that?

Before Rob and Finn moved in, that's when.

OH! It's no good – Mrs Robertson just doesn't understand what a FIASCO this family is turning into. I can't keep the promise I have made to her in my note (and myself in my diary): I am going to have to creep upstairs and find somewhere to hide and leave them all to it. Who was I kidding anyway? Mum is just cracking on with her new life, and no matter what Mrs Robertson says, she doesn't care what I think at all.

I let myself in, closing the door behind me as quietly as I can, but – just my luck – there is a lull in the noise from the kitchen just as the front door closes with a 'click'.

'Skye? Is that you?' Mum calls out. 'We're all in here!'

Really, Mum? I would never have known it.

I take a deep breath to steady myself and walk into the kitchen to see Yuki, Rob, Finn, Harris and Mum standing around, all still talking over each other. The argument seems to be about who is going to sit where.

'Hello, Skye,' Mum says wearily.

'Hi, what's up?' I ask, looking at everyone's fed-up expressions.

'Take a look,' Mum says, gesturing at the overcrowded room. There are six chairs squashed together around our kitchen table, and the plates and knives and forks are all touching each other. 'There is not enough room for six of us in this kitchen. The table only ever sat four, and now that Harris is getting bigger and Finn and you are both almost adult-sized—'

'Maybe we should bring that old table in from the garage and use it as an extension?' Rob says.

'There's no room for another table in here,' says Harris.

Mum plonks the water jug down in front of me. 'Exactly,' she says, shooting Rob a challenging look.

His mouth twists awkwardly. 'It's OK, Hellie. We can all just squoosh up a bit,' he says.

'Unless someone wants to eat in another room?' says Mum. She is still looking at Rob as she says this, but it is pretty clear that she really means she wants Yuki to leave the room.

I know that Yuki caused the flood, but Mum is really dragging out the resentment. It's not as if she is not accident-prone herself. And she can be just as absent-minded. She once left the kitchen taps running while she was talking to the postman, and when she came back in the floor was swimming in water. I know this because it is her favourite story, which she trots out every time Harris or I have not turned off the taps properly.

'Don't stress, Hellie,' Yuki says, taking the not very subtle hint. 'I don't need a chair. I will sit on the floor. It is better for your posture, you know. Especially as you get older,' she adds.

Mum's face tightens. I know that face: it is the one she uses when she is putting every ounce of her strength into not saying something she might regret. She has used it with me when she really wants to tell me off but can't because we are in a public place. It is usually followed by a fake, stretched smile, which does not reach her eyes, and a sarcastic comment. Rob seems to read Mum's expression too, because he goes to put his hands on her shoulders and says something to her, but I don't catch what it is because Yuki has started talking to Finn.

'So I was thinking, angel,' she says. 'How about you ask your band round here for a practice? I heard that the school hall is going to have to close soon for maintenance work?'

Finn freezes, his hand halfway to his open mouth with an overloaded fork. 'When did you hear that? I didn't know anything about that.'

I didn't either, I think. Effi didn't mention it.

'Well, I'm telling you, honey. The head told me when I was talking to him about the possibility of my running some meditation classes,' says Yuki. 'The hall is the perfect space for that, and you kids are so tense these days with the all academic pressure and the homework and—'

'NO, MUM!'

Yuki smiles and turns away from Finn, deftly changing the subject. 'So anyway, Rob was saying he has almost finished soundproofing your garage – isn't that right, lovely?' she says over her shoulder to Rob.

He looks up from whispering in Mum's ear. 'Hmm?' he says to Yuki.

Yuki rolls her eyes. 'You weren't listening. Never mind,' she says, waving her long fingers at him. 'What do you say, Finn?'

Finn's face is a picture. I can tell he is struggling with feeling annoyed about his mum's meditation class, and on the other hand he is excited about getting the band round to use the new soundproofed garage. It was kind of a bribe on Rob's part when they moved here: to give Finn drumming lessons and then to let him have the garage as a special place to play. Also in the past Yuki has tried to put him off playing the drums because she says it is not a calming instrument, so it is lovely of her to encourage him like this.

'OK,' he says.

Harris is bouncing up and down. 'Is that the Hogs?' he says, his eyes shining. 'Can I come and watch you practise?'

Finn reaches out and ruffles Harris's hair. 'Sure, buddy,' he says. Then he raises his eyebrows at me. 'Perhaps Skye would like to come, too. Effi will be there.'

'Oh. Yeah?' I say, reaching for the water, avoiding his gaze.

'Oh, *yeah*,' says Finn. He somehow manages to put more meaning than anyone would think possible into two small words. 'Would you like to see him?'

'I "see" him at school all time,' I say.

'Aha! You do? I thought there was something going on,' says Finn.

'What is that supposed to mean?' I say.

'Who's Effi?' Mum asks.

Yuki comes over and stands between me and Finn, resting a hand lightly on each of us. 'Hey, guuuuuys,' she says. 'If Skye has a crush, it is not cool to tease her, angel,' she says to Finn.

'Skye has a crush! Skye has a crush!' Harris chants.

'Shut UP!' I shout, leaning over to swipe at my brother.

I knock the water jug over and send the contents cascading down the table. Harris jumps back, shrieking, the front of his school shorts soaked, throwing his chair against Mum, who shrieks as well.

'I told you there wasn't enough room in here,' Mum cries. She grabs a cloth and begins vigorously wiping Harris down. 'The sooner we find somewhere else to live, the better. Rob – get those house details we were looking at, can you? They are on my desk. I think we should show the kids that place in Wotherington.'

'*Wotherington?*' I repeat. 'That's miles away!'

'It's pretty cool. It's near where we used to live,' says Finn.

'Cool!' Harris mimics, looking up at Finn adoringly.

'Well, that's nice for you!' I say. 'Why did you bother moving away from there if it was so *cool?*'

'Skye . . .' Mum starts in her warning tone.

'No! Don't say "Skye" like that,' I shout. I am hot with anger. 'This is my life too. I don't want to move. I want to stay here where my best friend lives and where my school is and where I can go and visit Mrs Robertson. And I do NOT want to go and live where Finn has loads of mates and I know NO ONE AT ALL!'

A voice inside my head is telling me to stop shouting

and to remember the promise I made to myself on the bus. I should be telling Mum about the conversation I had with Mrs Robertson; I should be saying that I do understand how life can be tricky, how change can sometimes be a good thing.

But all I can think is what I am now shouting at Mum, blood rushing to my head, my heart pounding: 'Are you listening to me? I DO NOT WANT TO MOVE!'

'OK, Skye, that's enough,' Mum snaps. 'Everyone be quiet and sit down, please. I think we are all tired. We need to get on with tea. Harris has to practise his lines before bed, and I don't want him staying up late.'

'Hellie, Hellie,' Yuki cuts across her. 'Always rushing.' She smiles sweetly and shakes her head. 'There is no rush to eat, and surely there's no rush to move house either? We can learn to give each other space. Time is a human construct – not something we should feel tied to. You need to hang loose and go with the flow a bit more.'

'Argh!' Mum cries, throwing her hands in the air. 'I've had enough. I really have. You do tea, Rob. I'm not hungry any more.' And she marches out of the room.

Which means I now can't. She has stolen my exit.

I glance at Finn. He looks mortified. His face is red and he is staring at the floor, drawing an imaginary picture with the toe of his trainer.

Harris looks stricken. 'Mum?' he shouts out of the

door. Then, when he doesn't get an answer, he runs out after her.

Rob is glaring at Yuki. 'Well done,' he says with heavy sarcasm.

Yuki looks at me and shrugs. 'Just saying,' she says. 'Things were getting heavy. And it wasn't the best way to bring up the move really, was it, honey . . . ?' She tails off as she sees Rob's face harden.

Finn rolls his eyes and leaves the room without a word.

Am I the only one who thinks Yuki has a point? Mum *is* always stressed these days. She probably should go with the flow. And she probably needs a few meditation classes too.

Anyway, I am just glad the conversation has moved away from us moving to Wotherington.

And from me and Effi.

Chapter Nineteen

I am in Harris's room. He is not back from school yet. Today is the day they hear who has got the parts in *The Wizard of Oz*. Rob has gone to get him because Mum is still at work and Yuki is out.

Rob and Mum announced last night that we were going to visit the house in Wotherington 'together – this weekend', because they think it is 'the right place for us' and that once we have seen it we 'will *love* it'. And then Mum made a point of saying that it would be very helpful if Yuki could stay behind and walk Pongo.

I tried saying that I would stay behind and walk Pongo, but Mum said that would 'defeat the object' of us going to see the house. She said (in her 'I am trying very hard to stay calm' voice) that I needed to have an open mind and that she knew I was worried, but that she also knew I would love the house. Yuki then said that if I didn't want to move, Mum should listen to my point of view, which I thought was very kind of her. Mum said Yuki should stay out of it, and then Yuki said, quite rightly if you ask me, that she could hardly stay out of it if she was being asked to be the family dog-sitter and general dogsbody (ha!) for the day, and that she was not going to do jobs like that for nothing.

Then Mum got angry and said that Yuki seemed to get an awful lot out of her and Rob for nothing, so maybe it would be nice for Yuki to give something in return. Yuki then offered to teach Mum some yoga, which I thought was an excellent idea as it might actually help Mum to be calmer and to think straight, which might then lead to her realizing that she shouldn't rush into the move and that she should LISTEN TO ME.

Mum has never been able to resist the idea of learning new things, and Yuki can be pretty persuasive, so I thought Mum might say, 'Thank you, Yuki, that would be lovely,' but actually what she said was, 'Over my dead body,' which

I thought was quite harsh. Yuki tried to make a joke about Mum doing the 'corpse pose', which is apparently a thing in yoga, but this did not go down well AT ALL.

I pointed out later to Yuki (once I was out of Mum's earshot) that Mum is not very supple or even that fit, so it might be hard for her to do yoga anyway.

'Don't worry, babe,' Yuki told me. 'Maybe she will come round to the idea if I give her space. I just wanted to share some peace and love with your mum. Restore the balance between us, you know? Yoga is not a competitive sport. It's all about listening to your body.'

I didn't know what she meant about 'listening to your body'. The only time I can hear what my body is saying is when my tummy is rumbling. Or worse. And I really don't like to think about the kind of noises Mum's body might start making once she tries to stand on her head or bend over backwards into a yoga pose. So maybe it's a good thing she refused.

I do wish Mum would calm down, though. I have not had a chance to get her on her own at all. I am so frustrated. When I got back from visiting Mrs Robertson, I really thought I had accepted Rob and Finn and the idea of our two families becoming one. Now I see that this was totally stupid. There is nothing good about our two families coming together. The way things are going, I don't suppose I will ever be able to have a one-to-one chat with Mum ever again. I am back to square one and wish with all my heart that Finn and Rob had never come into our lives.

I can wish as much as I like, though. It doesn't change anything. I might as well be invisible.

I haven't even been able to talk to Aubrey properly as she has been under a dark cloud for days. Zane apparently never did FaceTime her and is once again not replying to any of her messages, and this has sent her spiralling into a very bad mood. She goes around with her headphones on, even at lunchtime, listening to depressing love songs and telling anyone who will listen that they cannot possibly understand how broken-hearted she is. I have tried telling her that she needs to move on, but apparently there is no room in her life for anyone else but Zane. EVEN THOUGH HE LIVES ON ANOTHER CONTINENT!

She's right about one thing: I don't know much about being broken-hearted - but I certainly feel alone, and that must be almost as bad. I can't even bring myself to talk to Effi ever since the comments Finn and Harris made about me having a crush on him. I thought perhaps I had found a new friend who understood me because he has been through a move himself, but I can't talk to him now in case Finn sees us together. Oh no. I have just had a hideous thought: what if Finn has actually said something to him about me liking him? What if ALL THE HOGS have heard this and think I have some huge crush?

It is too cringe-making to even write about.

I think I am just going to have to lie low and PRAY that my best friend sees sense and comes out of her sad lurve-trance. She is my only hope.

As if in answer to the sentence I have just written, the doorbell rings. I get up from my beanbag to go and answer it when it rings again and again and my phone buzzes too. It is Aubrey. She has texted:

Am outside! Are you in? 😖

I am overjoyed that she has come round, but what on earth is she in such a panic about?

The doorbell rings again.

'OK! OK! I'm coming!' I yell, as I hurtle down the stairs.

The second I open the door Aubrey launches herself at me for a hug and manages to knock me against the door frame and stamp on my toes in her enthusiasm.

'Ow!' I whine.

'Sorrreee!' Aubrey says, springing back. 'I mean, I really truly am sorry. I have been a hopeless friend. Can you forgive me?'

I look into her eyes. They are brimming with tears. My heart gives a little flip and I think about how much I have missed talking to her and how I hate to see her upset.

'Of course I can forgive you, you dweeb! Best friends forever, remember?' I say, pulling out the necklace she gave me from under the neck of my T-shirt.

'Don't!' she wails. 'It reminds me of Zane!'

'OK.' I shove it back under my T-shirt and force away a niggle of irritation. I thought the necklaces were all about us. Never mind, Aubrey's here now, and I have missed her. I tell her so.

'It's sooooo good to see you,' I say. 'I've got so much to talk to you about—'

'I know! Me too,' she butts in. She takes a deep breath and begins talking at a hundred miles an hour. I turn and lead her upstairs, while rolling my eyes and smiling. This is Aubrey, back on form.

'I've been reading those agony aunt columns you and I were looking at back when you told me about your mum and Rob and stuff?' she is saying. 'And well, you know, they are FULL of excellent advice about how to move on from a bad breakup. I don't know why I didn't think of it before – '

Hmm, maybe if you had LISTENED TO YOUR BEST FRIEND . . .

'– I have even been messaging one of them on this online forum where you can tell the person about your problems and they answer, like, straight away! So I told them ALL about Zane and how mean he's been, dumping me then saying he'll FaceTime and then not – you know – and I got the best advice about how if a boy doesn't answer your texts then he is SOOOO not worth it, and so I have decided to live my own life and that is why I need to talk to you and I was wondering what you thought about going to see the Hogs together at their next practice which I think is on Friday and—WOW!'

She stops short and takes in the scene. We have reached

my flood-damaged bedroom. Thankfully the sight of it has distracted her enough to leave her speechless and wide-eyed.

'Yeah,' I say. 'So now you see why *I've* been so upset.' I know she hasn't really noticed how upset I have been, because she has been too busy being all depressed and hysterical about Zane, but I am determined to have my moment.

'Wow,' Aubrey says again. 'I DO see. It looks a LOT worse in real life. Your books!' She gives me a squeeze. 'I am so sorry. I have been a bad friend. I know you say you forgive me, but . . .' She pauses and looks at me, biting her bottom lip. 'I didn't realize it was this bad. So – you're not sleeping in here?'

I give a dry laugh. 'No. Take a look at this.' I lead her around Rob's tools and stepladder and the boxes that Mum has filled with the stuff I wasn't able to fit into Harris's room. We go over to the bookcases, which Rob has started pulling away from the wall so that he can take a look at the damage. I push against the plaster. There is already a hole in the wall, but when I push, more of it comes away.

'Holy moly!' Aubrey cries. 'You made a hole right the way through to next door! That is freaky.'

'Yeah well, not so freaky when you discover that the two houses were once one big one,' I say.

Aubrey's eyes are so wide they look as if they are about to pop. 'What?' she cries.

I can't help smiling. I've got her attention now.

'Come into Harris's room and I'll tell you,' I say.

We go and sit on Harris's bed, and Gollum comes in to join us. She only comes when Harris is out because he makes too much noise and annoys her. I pull her on to my lap and she starts purring like a jet engine.

I tell Aubrey about my visit to Mrs Robertson's and about the tense atmosphere at home since the flood and how Mrs Robertson reckons I just need to give Mum a chance, but how I can't because I never get time to talk to her – and I finish by telling her about the house in Wotherington, which we all have to visit this weekend.

As I talk, Aubrey listens and, for once, does not try to interrupt or give any advice or comment. In fact, as I talk, I notice that Aubrey seems to be concentrating extremely hard as though she is trying to work out a tricky maths problem. She is frowning and nodding as I speak. I have just got to the bit about the new house and how I have recently had the feeling I didn't think Mum wanted to leave this place, when Aubrey makes me jump.

'Wait a minute!' she shouts, leaping up from the bed.

Gollum hisses and sticks her claws into my thighs.

'Hey!' I say to Gollum, then, 'Aubrey, you scared us!'

Aubrey is standing in front of me, staring into my eyes, her face lit up with excitement. 'But don't you see! You have the most perfect solution to every single one of your problems RIGHT HERE!'

'Aubrey, you are not making sense and you are acting like an insane person,' I say.

'NO! You're the one who's not making sense,' she says. 'You say you don't want to move and that you think your mum doesn't want to. You say you guys don't have enough room here. You show me the hole in the wall. You tell me Mrs Robertson used to own the whole house –'

'Yes, I know, but what does this have to do with a solution?'

'LISTEN! The two houses USED TO BE ONE HOUSE,' Aubrey says.

'I know, I just told you that – OH!' and suddenly I see what she is saying. 'You mean . . . you think I should tell Mum and Rob . . . No, but that is such a huge job . . . they would never . . .'

'SKYE!' Aubrey cries. 'You HAVE to tell them. Rob knows all about building houses, he is doing the repairs here anyway, right? I bet he could knock the two back together again.'

I very much doubt it is as easy as Aubrey is making it sound, but I can't help feeling excited. The fizzing feeling I had when I left Mrs Robertson has come back.

'Yuki did say that the flood was a sign . . .' I am almost talking to myself as I replay what Yuki actually said on the night of the flood. 'She said, "The bath overflowing, the hole in the wall – this is totally cosmic karma!"'

'What does that mean?' Aubrey says.

'Well, at the time I didn't know,' I confess. 'But she kept saying things like we needed to "go with the flow of life". And then Mrs Robertson said that stuff about "new beginnings" and she winked. Do you think she was actually hinting at this? I think you're right, Aubrey,' I say, as the idea grows on me. 'I think it's meant to be: our two houses WANT to go back into one!'

Chapter Twenty

'We need to tell everyone as soon as they get home,' Aubrey says, pulling me up from the bed. She whirls me around in a circle. We are both giggling.

The realization that we might not have to move away is filling my head as though someone is pumping up a balloon full of helium inside my brain. I want to laugh and shout and float up into the sky.

We dance out of Harris's room and on to the landing and we're singing and shouting and generally behaving like the loony best friends we have always been and I am feeling that I am on top of the world, when the front door is flung open and I hear Finn shout, 'Anyone home?'

He looks up and sees us on the landing before I have a chance to grab Aubrey and run back into Harris's room.

'Hey, Finn!' Aubrey shouts, waving manically. 'Hey, Effi!'

No. Not Effi, too! Why is he here?

'Shut up, Aubrey,' I mutter. This is the last thing I need. I have just got my best friend's full attention for the first time in days, we have moved away from talking non-stop about boyfriends, and now Aubrey's ex-crush walks in. Not to mention Effi, who always seems to make me do the weirdest things.

'What?' says Aubrey, looking puzzled. 'I thought you liked Effi?' she says – far too loudly, in my opinion. Then she pushes past me and makes her way down the stairs. 'Are you guys going to practise here?' she is saying to Finn, looking over his shoulder to see if the rest of the Hogs are here, probably. I wish she wasn't such a groupie.

Effi is smiling at me as I come down after Aubrey. Well, I can't exactly NOT come down now that he has seen me.

'Hello, Skye,' he says. 'I have not seen you for a few days. Finn and I were on the same bus. He asked me here to hang out for a while. I hope you don't mind?'

As he says this, I reach the last step and trip. I lose my balance and crash into Aubrey, who shrieks and jumps to the right, leaving me to fall head-first into Effi.

'There she goes, throwing herself at you again, Effi,' says Finn, laughing.

I disentangle myself, desperately trying to think of a smart comeback, when Rob walks in through the still-open front door, a wailing Dorothy-slash-Harris holding his hand, and Mum, looking anxious, comes in behind them.

Part of me is grateful for the distraction. Maybe Harris dressed as Dorothy in full-on meltdown mode is enough to take the attention away from me and Effi. But when Harris's wailing goes up a notch, my stomach drops as I realize just how unhappy my little brother really is.

'What's up, Harris buddy?' Finn asks, putting his hand on Harris's shoulder.

'Oh Harris,' I say, bending to give him a hug. 'If those bullies have had a go at you again, they will have me AND Finn to reckon with this time.'

'And me!' Aubrey chips in.

'It's not that,' Harris whimpers. He pushes past me and throws his arms around Finn. 'The teachers won't let me be Dorotheeeeeeeeey!' he cries, burying his face in Finn's stomach.

'Oh boy,' Finn says. He gives Harris's head an awkward pat.

We all look at each other. Rob looks awkward. Effi and Aubrey look puzzled. Mum's face is ashen.

'That's appalling!' she says. 'I will go in with you tomorrow and find out exactly what their problem is. I doubt any other child knows all the words to the songs.

And I bet no one else has their own real live Pongo – I mean, Toto.'

'No,' says Harris. 'I don't want to be in the stupid show now anyway.'

'Hey, guys! What's going on?'

Mum's expression darkens and she shakes her head at Rob, mouthing something that looks like, 'Seriously?' at him.

Yuki takes one look at the sniffing, sobbing Harris and says, 'Oh I'm sorry, baby. Did you not get the part? Well, maybe it's for the best. I don't think a boy has ever played Dorothy before.' She laughs.

No one joins in.

Harris removes himself from Finn's stomach to growl at Yuki. 'I am NOT a baby,' he says. And then, ripping the ribbon out of his hair, he takes a huge breath and wails, 'Waaaaaah!' – which rather disproves his point.

'OK, I can see now is not a good time for us to have that yoga session then, Hellie?' Yuki says.

'Yes, you're right; now is not a good time. In fact, it is *never* a good time,' says Mum in a dangerous tone. 'I have told you already: I – don't – want – to – do – yoga – with – you.' She says this very slowly and very menacingly. I have never seen Mum look so thunderous. 'In fact—'

'Yuki,' Rob says. 'Skye, Aubrey, could you maybe

take Harris upstairs? And boys –' he looks at Finn and Effi – 'why don't you go round to ours? I left some biscuits there while I was working on the bathroom. You can show Effi the garage, Finn?' he adds.

'Sure. C'mon, Effi,' Finn says with a scowl. 'Anything to be out of here.'

Effi looks relieved to be leaving the madhouse too. I can't blame him. They make a hasty exit.

I am torn between wanting to run after them and being glad that they have gone. What is wrong with me?

Aubrey whispers, 'Should I go too?'

'No way,' I whisper back. 'I need you!'

I am about to take Harris by the hand and lead him away, when Yuki sighs loudly.

'Harris, honey, maybe this whole thing is meant to be, you know? Society is so hung up on traditional gender roles. I don't think the kind of school you've chosen for Harris is ready for a boy to be Dorothy. And – well, look at those shoes on you—'

Harris kicks off his ruby-red slippers and lets out a furious howl.

Rob stands between Yuki and Harris and hisses, 'Leave it, Yuki.' Then turning to me he says, 'Take him upstairs, please. Now.'

'Actually, Rob – and Mum, I really need to talk to you,' I say. 'Aubrey and I have been—'

'Skye, not now . . .' Mum shoots me a warning look.

I give her a look back, but I do as Rob has asked, and Aubrey follows us up the stairs in silence.

'Aren't you going to say something?' Aubrey says when we get to Harris's room. 'You need to tell them about the house. And I want to be there when you do!'

'I know. I KNOW!' I say. I have to raise my voice above Harris, who is sobbing again and asking for Bop-Bop, his comfort blanket – something he hasn't done since last term when he was being bullied.

'Everyone laughed at me!' Harris is wailing. 'Even some of the teachers did. They say I have to be the Lion,' he says, fresh tears welling in his eyes. 'I don't want to be the Cowardly Lion!' His voice rises as the tears fall. 'I AM NOT A COWARD.'

'No, you are not,' I say.

'In fact, you are braver than most boys I know,' says Aubrey.

At that moment, Mum appears in the doorway. She hands Harris his ratty old Bop-Bop and says, 'There, there, little bean.'

Mum and I exchange an anxious glance.

'Poor poppet,' says Mum. 'He had learned all the lines and the songs, Aubrey.'

'And I really, really, really wanted to wear Mum's shoes!' Harris says.

'They are lovely shoes,' Aubrey says.

I roll my eyes at her. That is not going to cheer him up, is it?

'What?' she says. 'They are! Just saying . . .'

'You know what,' I say to Harris. 'Why don't we look at the book version of the story? I think it's a bit different from the film. I bet the Lion is a much more important part than you realize. Mrs Robertson gave me the book.' I shoot a hasty look at Aubrey, and she nods encouragingly. 'Actually, talking of Mrs Robertson, Aubrey and I have got something amazing to tell you and Mum—'

'I don't care about the stupid book!' Harris shouts, and stamps his foot. 'I wanted to wear those shoes, and Mum was going to make the dress all sticky-outy with that special scratchy tutu stuff, and I wanted to fly and have Pongo in my arms all the time like Dorothy has Toto in her arms in the film.' He throws himself on to his bed and puts Bop-Bop over his head.

I am about to point out that Pongo is a Labrador who weighs at least twenty-seven kilos, and that carrying him around onstage might prove problematic, but Mum has read my mind and is shaking her head vigorously.

'Hello?' says a voice.

It's Effi. He is peeping round the door.

'Oh, hello,' says Mum, forcing a smile. 'You and Finn

need a drink or something?' she asks.

Effi smiles back and shakes his head. 'No thank you, Mrs Green,' he says. 'I was talking to Finn about Harris's disappointment and I had an idea. Can I come in?'

Aubrey nudges me and giggles. I scowl at her.

Mum raises her eyebrows at me in a knowing way and says, 'Of course you can.'

'Where's Finn?' Harris asks.

'He is talking with his parents,' says Effi. 'Mr Parker told me that they have some important things to discuss. I think I was getting in the way.'

'Ah,' says Mum. 'Well, you are welcome to stay here for as long as you like.' She looks at me again as she says this.

'What?' I say. She is annoying me. I feel hot and awkward and I wish she would go away and stop looking at me as though to say, 'Skye's got a friend who's a BOY!' which is I'm sure what she means by all those knowing glances.

'Nothing!' says Mum. 'I'll leave you to it, then.'

Aubrey giggles again. 'Shall I "leave you to it" as well?' she says.

'Shut UP!' I hiss.

Mum raises her eyebrows again, but thankfully goes.

Effi sits down on Harris's bed. 'I am very sorry you have had a bad day,' he says kindly. 'I wonder if there is something I can do to help you. Have you ever read the book *The Wonderful Wizard of Oz* by L. Frank Baum? It is the story on which the film was based, but it's very different, you know.'

'H-how do *you* know about the book?' I ask. 'I thought you liked sci-fi?' I immediately feel stupid for saying this. As if a person can't like reading more than one kind of book.

'How do you know what books Effi likes?' Aubrey asks, suspiciously.

'Skye is right, I do,' Effi says, nodding. 'We have talked about this in the library at school, Aubrey. How are you getting on with *HG2G*, Skye?'

I can't answer him. I know that I have gone so red now that I have to turn and pretend to tidy up some clothes that are on the floor.

'I don't know what you are talking about and I don't know the book of the Wizard of Oz and I don't want to. I just told Skye that,' Harris says, sulkily. 'I love the film and I love Dorothy and I want to be her!' His face crumples again.

'That's OK,' Effi says hastily. He scoots closer to Harris and puts an arm around him. 'I just wanted to tell you that the Lion turns out to be a hero in the end, doesn't he? And in the book he is even more courageous than in the movie.'

Harris gives a hiccuppy sob and a big sniff.

'Told you. Effi is right,' I say quietly, without looking round.

I don't trust myself to say any more. My tummy is flipping and turning, and my brain is splitting in two again: half of it wants Effi to leave, and half of it wants him to stay.

'Tell us more about the Lion, Effi,' Aubrey says.

I glance at her to see if she is teasing, but to be fair she does actually look interested.

Effi beams. 'The Lion is a wonderful character, Skye,' he says, looking at me. 'Do you have a copy? I know you have a lot of books.'

'Yes. I – I think it's in one of these boxes,' I say, and I start rummaging. 'Can you help me, Aubrey?' I ask.

We start unloading my boxes of books. I am just so grateful to have something to do that doesn't involve looking at or talking to Effi.

I only hope Aubrey can manage not to say anything embarrassing in front of him.

Chapter Twenty-One

We find the book eventually. It is scuffed and damaged, but Harris doesn't seem to mind. He is already a lot calmer now that he has the prospect of Effi giving him some attention.

'So, shall I read to you from where the Lion comes in, Harris?' Effi says. 'Or would one of you like to? Skye? Aubrey?' he asks us in turn.

'Actually, *I* think I'm going to *get some drinks*,' says Aubrey with a weird amount of emphasis. I frown at her. She locks eyes with me.

'OK,' says Effi. 'I will do it.' He sits down on Harris's bed, next to Harris.

'Yay!' Harris scoots along to get closer to Effi as he leafs through the book to get to the right place.

Aubrey clears her throat loudly. 'Ahem.' Then she nods towards Effi and gives me another intense look.

'Why are you looking at me like that?' I ask.

Aubrey rolls her eyes, then stares at me again – her eyes even wider – and nods towards Effi again.

'What?' I say.

She lets out an exasperated noise and leaves the room.

Sometimes I think my best friend lives in a world of her own.

Luckily Effi's idea seems to work like magic. Harris is back to his cheery, bouncy self.

'Listen to this, Skye!' he says. 'Listen to what the Wizard says to the Lion!' and he takes the book from Effi and reads: '"You have plenty of courage, I am sure . . . All you need is confidence in yourself. There is no living thing that is not afraid when it faces danger. The true courage is in facing danger when you are afraid, and that kind of courage you have in plenty." Isn't that right?'

'Told you,' I say, smiling.

'You know what I think?' Effi says. 'You are already full of courage, Harris.'

'I am?' Harris says.

'Yes!' says Effi. 'I think you are very brave to have done the audition in the first place.'

Harris grins and bounces vigorously on the bed. 'Yay!' he says, punching the air. 'I am BRAVE!'

I realize Effi is right and that he is not just saying this to make Harris feel better.

He is very sincere when he says to Harris, 'I bet loads of those people who were laughing were actually *jealous* of you, Harris. You had so much confidence. In fact, I am sure that is the real reason the teachers want you to be the Lion. In my country the Lion is the king of the animals, you know? And I think you will make a great king!'

Even if Effi is only saying this to be nice, it doesn't matter. It works. Harris is squealing with delight now.

'You know what I also think, Harris?' Effi said, as my brother leans against him, looking at the pictures in the book. 'I think you will make a very handsome Lion. We could help make you an amazing costume. Wouldn't you love to have a huge fluffy mane and a long swishy tail?'

'YES!' Harris cries. 'I know just how to make those as well. Mum has a gold feather boa that would make a brilliant lion's mane – do you think she will let me cut it up?'

I look at Effi, and we laugh.

'I don't know, Harris. You will have to ask her,' Effi says.

'Effi, you are my new best friend!' Harris cries, grabbing him and hugging him. I don't know why, but that makes me blush.

Just at that moment, Aubrey comes in with some cans of drink, and Finn is with her.

Finn says, 'Hey! What about me? I thought I was your best buddy!'

Harris responds by whirling Bop-Bop above his head, charging at Finn and rugby-tackling him (which is quite awkward to watch, as he is still wearing his Dorothy dress).

The pair of them fall to the floor and start their usual game of wrestling and giggling and tickling. Normally this annoys me, but it is so good to see Harris happy again that I find myself smiling.

'Thanks,' I say quietly to Effi.

'It worked then?' Aubrey says, opening a can and handing it to me.

'Yes. Harris is now convinced that being the Lion is a good thing,' I say.

'Thanks to Effi!' says Aubrey, giving me one of her freaky, intense looks again.

'Finn is very good with your brother,' Effi says, watching them chase each other down the landing. He looks back at me. 'You know, I think your families will be fine together. You do not need to worry about it. And I have to tell you, I am very happy we moved here now that I have met Finn and you. My only hope is that you will not have to move so far away that you will change schools.'

I feel my stomach plummet when he says this: it has

reminded me about the house Mum wants us to see.

'Uh-huh,' I say. I don't seem to be able to form any normal words. I pick up the can to take a sip as an excuse not to have to talk and – I miss my mouth completely! The drink goes all down my front. I am paralysed, praying that Finn will not look up and see.

Aubrey is giggling so hard she has to sit down.

What is wrong with me? I am beginning to think I have some kind of brain disorder that only clicks in whenever Effi is around. I am SO clumsy whenever I see him, and I just don't understand why.

'I will get a towel,' says Effi.

'What are you like?' Aubrey says, while Effi is gone.

'Shut up!' I say. I am cross with her for laughing, but I am even more cross with myself for being such an idiot.

'You must really like him,' Aubrey says.

'What do you mean?' I snap.

'It's obvious, isn't it?' Aubrey says. 'You are crushing on Effi big time!'

'No!' I protest. 'I just like him, that's all.'

'You are joking me!' says Aubrey. 'You can't *speak* properly when you are around him, you can't walk in a straight line and you can't even drink a can of Coke!'

'So what? I know I've been clumsy—'

'Seriously?' Aubrey cuts in. 'You haven't worked out

why you keep doing all that stuff? It's so obvious,' she says again.

I am about to get really angry and tell her to leave me alone, when she says, 'I don't know why you're stressing so much – he really likes you, too.'

At that moment Effi comes back with a towel, so I can't say anything back to Aubrey. She is looking as pleased with herself as Gollum does when she's caught a mouse. She always loves getting the last word.

'Sorry I was so long,' says Effi. 'I did not know where to look.' He catches me glaring at Aubrey and says, 'Oh, have I made you angry?'

'N-no,' I say, feeling my face go red again. 'Aubrey and I were just – having a misunderstanding.'

Effi looks troubled. 'What were you talking about?'

I open my mouth to say something random, but Aubrey gets in first.

'We were talking about how Skye's mum wants them to move to Wotherington,' she says.

I shake my head at her and mouth, 'What?'

But she carries on. 'I don't want Skye to move that far away – what about you, Effi?'

What is she up to? If she DARES to say anything about me having a crush!

'But I was saying,' Aubrey continues, 'why doesn't Rob knock the two houses together so that they can stay here?' Aubrey puts her hand on her hip, and raises her eyebrows at me.

'That is an excellent idea! Can people do that?' Effi says, his face shining.

'I – I don't know,' I say, avoiding Aubrey's gaze. 'But I was telling Aubrey – I know the lady who lived in Finn's place before. She's in a home now. I visited her and she told me the two houses used to be one big house.'

'Yes – so I said, why don't they just put it back together again?' Aubrey says.

Effi laughs. 'Your friend Aubrey is a very clever girl, Skye. Does Finn know about this? Have you told your mother? You must tell everyone straight away!'

Finn and Harris crash through the door as Effi says this.

'Tell everyone what?' Finn asks, breathless from his play fight with Harris.

Aubrey tells him the whole story, and as she explains, a wide grin spreads across Finn's face.

'This is AWESOME!' he cries, picking Harris up and throwing him dangerously close to the ceiling. 'Dad will love this idea. We have to go and find him and Hellie and tell them now!'

Chapter Twenty-Two

Rob and Mum were super-excited when we told them what Mrs Robertson had said. Rob said he could not believe he hadn't thought of the idea himself, and he went around our house, pointing at things and saying random builder-type stuff like, 'Of COURSE it was one house! Why didn't I notice it before? Look at the ceiling here - see that coving? It disappears at the edge and isn't finished properly. You can actually SEE the houses were joined if you look carefully. There are loads of clues . . .'

(I didn't know what 'coving' was, but apparently it's the curved bit around the edge of the ceiling. Normally it runs all the way around the edge of the room in a house like ours, but it actually doesn't, because it's been cut in two!)

Mum was a little more cautious and kept saying boring grown-up things like, 'What about planning? Do we have to speak to the council?' and, of course, 'How much will it cost?'

But Rob assured her that if the house had been one complete house before, then it should not be a problem to get permission to put it back the way it once was. He was practically dancing around the kitchen with excitement, saying it would be a 'great project' and it would give us 'so much more value for our money'. (Mum liked that bit.)

Finn and Harris and I were more excited about our rooms. Finn reckoned he would be getting a room double the size of his old one, and Harris was planning how he would decorate his in a Wizard of Oz theme, with a Yellow Brick Road carpet. I was just looking forward to not having to share with Harris the Lion any more. (Since he decided that being the Lion was a good thing, he has been singing all the time, not to mention *roaring* at every opportunity and practising prancing around and flicking his 'tail' at everyone. The tail is half of Mum's gold feather boa – she said he could cut it up and use half for the mane and half for the tail. This means that I have twice had the fright of my life when I have been walking through the house, minding my own business, only to have Harris jump out at me from behind a door, roaring and twitching his 'tail' in my face. I will be glad when this show is over.)

Aubrey brought up the subject of parties, which I thought Mum would go mental about, but she actually laughed and said it would be 'wonderful to fill the house with all our friends'. She said, 'We should definitely have a massive housewarming when it's all done.' Finn got really excited at that and said he and Effi would get the band to play.

Rob pointed out that it would take a long time to sort things out, and that it would be 'chaos' while the building work was going on.

No one cared about that though. And let's face it - life can't get much more chaotic than it is right now, can it?

At least the excitement over the house distracted Aubrey from going on at me about Effi.

It hasn't stopped me thinking about what she said, though. I would never admit this out loud to anyone - but I think she is right. I think

I do have a crush on Effi. (I can't believe I have just written that down - it makes it feel more real!) This is very worrying. What if I go completely brain-dead like Aubrey did over Finn last term - not to mention Zane? I don't want to turn into a lurved-up loony who can only think about boys. Or one boy, anyway.

The thing is, I think I am already beyond hope, because I can't stop thinking about him.

I will have to just hope and pray that he never finds out.

Meanwhile, the house is the thing everyone else is thinking about all the time. Mum made Rob promise that he would talk to Yuki about it. She has been lying low since Harris came back from his audition. I don't blame her. She probably values her eardrums too much. The noise he made that evening! Plus she is a calm person who loves peace, and there hasn't been much of that around here lately. If ever.

Anyway, Mum and Rob have called yet another 'family meeting' for tomorrow. Rob went to the council today and got hold of the old plans and spoke to the person in charge of all that stuff, and he is going to explain it to us all over tea.

Chapter Twenty-Three

We are all sitting in our squashed positions around
the kitchen table. Yuki has been very quiet, other than
complimenting Mum on her vegetarian pasta bake,
which I think is mega-kind of her, as personally I think
it tastes like glue. (Not that I have ever tasted glue, but
I am thinking of the flavour in a metaphorical way to
basically say the food is disgusting.) I am sure Yuki is not
really enjoying it, as I have been watching her picking
bits out of it and dropping them down to a very grateful
Pongo when she thinks no one is looking.

I wish Pongo would come over to my side of the table
so that I can do the same thing.

Rob and Mum are chattering away about nothing in
particular while Mum fills up everyone's drinks; Finn
is texting under the table; and I am getting bored and
wondering when this whole 'family meeting' thing is
actually going to start.

Harris is singing to himself. Thankfully he is doing this softly, as Mum has told him off twice already for singing loudly at the table.

I try to catch Harris's eye to tell him to shut up, when he suddenly blurts out, 'Yuki, who is Neville?'

All eyes turn on Yuki. She freezes right in the middle of picking out more of the pasta bake to give to Pongo. Then she seems to make an effort to pull herself together, and fixing a smile on her face she says, 'What's that, sweetie?'

'Don't call me sweetie,' says Harris. Then he sits up and says, 'I said "who is Neville?"'

Yuki clears her throat and looks at her plate. 'I – I don't know anyone called Neville,' she says. 'I don't know why you're asking me this.'

'Yuki . . .' Rob says, his voice low.

Yuki snaps her head up to look at him. 'What?' she says. She sounds very different from her usual peaceful self.

'What's going on?' Finn asks.

Mum is looking puzzled.

Yuki suddenly turns on Harris. 'What were you doing? Were you spying on me?' she says, her voice hard.

Harris shrugs. 'I wasn't,' he says.

'You must have been,' Yuki says.

'I wasn't spying on you. You were making a lot of noise, shouting at Neville down the phone. I could hear you through the wall. Why are you angry with him? And why do you have to give the car back?'

Yuki rises out of her seat and leans over the table, squaring up to Harris. Mum gasps and Rob gets up and puts a hand on Yuki's arm, but she is already hissing at Harris, 'That is NONE of your business, you little—'

'That's enough,' Rob cuts in, pulling her gently back. 'I am sure Harris is sorry that he was eavesdropping. Aren't you, Harris?' he asks, pointedly.

Harris pulls a face. 'Not really,' he says. 'She was mean about me not getting to be Dorothy.' Then he sees Rob's expression and slumps back in his chair and mutters, 'Sorry.'

I have never seen Yuki like this before. She looks like a boiling pot about to blow its lid.

'This is not cool, Rob,' she says. 'A person should be allowed some privacy. It's not as if I don't give you and Hellie space, is it?'

'Well, actually . . .' Mum begins, but Rob gives her a look, so she tails off.

'Like, I know it's not ideal us all being squashed into this house,' Yuki goes on, 'but once you have fixed your bathroom, we can go back to yours, can't we, Rob? And then everyone will have more personal space, and it will give us time to find the right house – I know you like that one in Wotherington, but it's not exactly perfect, location-wise, is it?'

Mum widens her eyes at Rob and sits back, her arms folded. 'You can't be serious – haven't you told her—?'

'Yeah – about that, Yuki,' Rob says quickly.

He takes a deep breath and begins telling her about the plans to knock the houses together. 'I wanted to tell you before tonight,' Rob says, 'but you've not been easy to get hold of these past couple of days, and then I was out all day today . . .'

I feel as though all the air has been sucked out of the room. Yuki's face goes through a wide range of expressions. Then she leaps up and rushes at Rob. I am worried she is going to hit him or something, but instead she squeals and throws her arms around his neck.

'You guys!' she exclaims. 'This is GREAT news. So much better than moving house. We'll have so much more space and it'll be great for Finn to stay in the area and not move again now that he has the band and his mates and—'

'Stop,' Rob says, wriggling free of her grasp.

Yuki backs off, looking hurt. 'What?' she asks.

Rob looks at Mum. 'Yuki,' he says. 'You can't stay with us forever, you know that.'

'Yeah, Mum,' Finn adds, surprising everyone. 'It's great that you want to spend time with us, but you don't live with us any more. You left, remember? And now Dad and Hellie are getting together. And – well, it's kind of freaky having you around all the time after years of not seeing you.' He looks embarrassed as he said this. 'I mean – it's like having three parents who actually live together. It's just weird. It's not normal.'

I feel kind of proud of him for saying what he thinks. Although I am not sure I would call my family in any way 'normal' any more.

'Yeah,' Harris chips in. 'Anyway, if you have this Neville person calling you and asking you to go back to wherever, then it's OK, isn't it? And you did promise you would give him his car back and pay him back his money—'

'What does all this mean, Yuki?' Rob interrupts. 'Who is this person and why do you have his car and how come you don't have any money?'

Yuki crumples. She sits down very suddenly, like a puppet whose strings have been cut. Her arms flop to her sides and her head falls forward, her long shiny hair shielding her face.

Then she puts her hands up and buries her face in them and mumbles something.

Rob's face softens and he shoots Mum an anxious glance. She rolls her eyes, which I think is pretty insensitive, given the situation.

'Tell me what *is* going on?' he asks, bending down and putting his hands on Yuki's shoulders.

She shrugs them off – then sitting up, she lets out a big sigh.

'I guess I am going to have to tell you. I was going to have to sooner or later.' She pauses. 'Neville's my guru,' she says. 'And . . . well, he was . . .' she hesitates. 'I don't know what to say! The thing is, we were not connecting any more. I couldn't create when I was in his presence. I had to get away. I needed space.'

'Tell me about it,' says Mum.

Yuki nods. 'Yeah, I needed some time out, so I – I sold our van to save money. And I kind of – borrowed Nev's car. I'm sorry!' she says, as Finn and Rob gasp. 'I know the van was ours, but I needed the cash so that I could get away. And then I thought, well, I should come to see you guys for a while – and, well, the truth is, being with you has made me realize I can't go back to the ashram now. I need to start over,' Yuki says. 'I came here to work things out, but when I got here and saw that you were all about to start over yourselves, moving house and everything, well, I couldn't let that happen, could I? Where would I go? You're not really going to chuck me out on to the street, are you?'

Rob looks at Mum, and Mum looks away.

'No,' he says finally. 'No, we wouldn't do that. Would we, Hellie?'

This family! Why does everything have to be such a fiasco?

The Final Chapter in My

Mortifying Life – No, Really

As Dorothy says in the book *The Wonderful Wizard of Oz*: 'If I ever go looking for my heart's desire again, I won't look any further than my own back yard.'

I said this to Aubrey, and she nudged me in the ribs and said, 'So Effi's your heart's desire, is he?'

I told her to shut up, and that what I meant was it was so funny that, in the end, Mum and Rob's perfect home had been right in front of their eyes the whole time, and that it took Yuki's disastrous flood to make them realize it! They didn't need to go looking for a new home miles away in a new place, when all the time our new home was right here, in our 'own back yard'.

As for Effi, well, yes, I am spending more

time with him. But only because we have been recommending each other books. He is now totally into the Philip Pullman His Dark Materials trilogy, and I have been reading a really old-fashioned science-fiction book called *Trillions* by Nicholas Fisk, which Effi gave me. He told me it was a 'late birthday present'. It is an amazing story about hordes of tiny aliens that look like jewels - so not your average alien monsters at all.

We asked Mrs Ball if we could start up a book club in the library. Mrs Ball is mega-excited about it because a lot of the older boys are coming along now that Effi has shown people how cool reading can be. Even Finn comes sometimes, which means Aubrey does too. (She says she is 'so over him', but since being dumped by Zane, she seems pretty happy whenever she gets the chance to hang out with Finn. Which is quite a lot now that he is basically my older brother.)

I need to make something clear, here: Effi and I are NOT boyfriend/girlfriend. Not how Aubrey imagines, anyway. Not yet . . . (EMBARRASSING THOUGHT ALERT!)

I do get to see Effi a lot, but that's mainly

because of the book club and the fact that the Hogs have been practising round here on a Friday ever since the school hall was closed for refurbishment. Yuki was telling the truth about that.

It was about the only thing she was telling the truth about, though.

She had actually run away from Neville without telling him where she was going. He was furious because she had basically *stolen* his car. Turns out he was not her 'guru' at all; he was her boyfriend! He had gone to the ashram in search of a new life after his career as a surf instructor hadn't worked out. Mum said it sounded as though they were 'just as flaky as each other - made for each other, in fact'. I would have stood up for Yuki, only I was beginning to get the distinct impression that she had caused the flood on purpose as a way of trying to stop Mum and Rob moving in together so that she would still have a roof over her head. And I am not sure I can forgive her that quickly for ruining my books. I have not got the guts to say anything though. I have just stopped wearing the bangles she gave me in a kind of silent protest instead.

Anyway, she is lucky that Rob is so kind. Thankfully she is not living with us any more. That was all getting far too 'heavy', as she would say. Rob has found her a flat in town and also got her a job so that she has enough money to pay for it. She is now giving art classes and teaching yoga and meditation in the evenings. Finn said he had never seen his mum work so hard, but I guess she doesn't have much choice. At least she is teaching the things that she loves. She comes round for meals sometimes. She has given Mum a few cookery lessons and shown her how to make sushi, which we all love. So, slowly but surely we are all learning to get along.

Rob has been working on knocking our houses together for nearly three months now. It has been very messy and we have all been squashed into a few rooms, but he is so clever at dividing things up with special boards and sheeting and stuff, that we have at least been able to carry on living here and have not had to move out all together while the work's been going on. Of course he hasn't done it on his own: he's had a team of builders in who are working for him. But he is the one who has designed the new layout. It is going to be so cool when it is finished! I am going to have an ATTIC ROOM! (Hashtag total luxury!) And I will have lovely new bookcases, wall to wall. So I will have a proper writer's garret, all to myself. Who knows? One day I might actually write my first proper book up there!

For now, though, I am still sharing with Harris, so I don't get much time or privacy to write. But it's OK. I have kind of got used to sharing with him - and I never thought I would say this, but it has actually been fun helping him get ready for the show.

We went to see it last night. Mrs Robertson came too! She is so chuffed about the house. She has made us promise to invite her to the housewarming. I told her the Hogs would be playing - I thought I had better warn her - and she beamed and said, 'I love a bit of live music!' She is amazing.

And Harris was amazing, too, as the Lion. Effi was right: the character did suit him. He was brave, auditioning to be Dorothy and not caring what people thought. He was also brave confronting Yuki with what he overheard. Who knows how things would have turned out if we had not found out that Yuki was really homeless? She would never have had the chance of a fresh start with Rob's help, because she was never going to be honest enough to admit that she needed it.

I also think that maybe there are some similarities between Dorothy and me that I had not seen before. She got cross with her family, just like I do. But she ended up going on a weird and wonderful journey, which was not something she had planned. OK, so not all of the journey was fun, and she argued with her new friends along the way as well. But in the end, she learned a lot about herself.

I have been on a kind of journey: one of self-discovery. I have learned that being thirteen is actually not that bad. I have learned that it is OK to have a crush on a boy and that it doesn't need to end in heartache and disaster, because you can actually get a new friend out of it.

But, most importantly, what I have learned

on my journey is that it is OK when things don't stay exactly the same. You don't need your house to stay the same. You don't even need your neighbours to stay the same. And you don't need your family to stay exactly the same. If Finn and Rob hadn't moved next door, I doubt I would ever have got to know Effi. Without Rob, Mum would not be as happy as she is today. And without Yuki's interfering, we would never have ended up with our fantastic new house.

Finally, without Mrs Robertson, we would not even have our new home. When she said, 'Some endings are actually beginnings in disguise,' she was so right. I found out from Mrs Ball that a mystic philosopher of ancient China called Lao Tzu said something very similar. He said:

'New beginnings are often disguised as painful endings.'

Funny, because it's the kind of thing you might have expected Yuki to say. But people aren't always what they seem to be. A Scarecrow (or a best friend!) without a brain might turn out to be the brainiest person of all; a Tin Man without a heart might turn out to show the most love for everyone; and the most cowardly Lion might very well turn out to be the bravest of the bunch.

And home might be where you least expect to find it. But I know one thing for certain - and I'm with the Dorothy of the film version of *Oz* on this one - 'There's no place like home.'*

[*In the book, it is another character that uses those words. Dorothy actually says, 'take me home to Aunt Em'. Just saying.]

Anna Wilson used to edit children's books until she discovered it was much more fun to write them. She took a flying leap from being an editor to being a fully-fledged author in 2008 and has never looked back (except when she has tripped over something). Inspired by her family, friends and pets, she writes funny yet heart-warming novels which are absolutely NOT based on any MORTIFYINGLY EMBARRASSING incidents which have happened to her in the past.*

Anna lives in Bradford on Avon with her husband, two children and an array of pets including a dog, cats, a tortoise and a pair of extremely noisy ducks.

*This may not be entirely true.